# *Wait for True Love*

# *Wait for True Love*

Faithe Hoover Musser

Second Edition

All rights reserved, including the right of
reproduction in whole or in part in any form.

Copyright © 1997 by Faithe Hoover Musser

Manufactured in the United States of America
ISBN: 0-533-11974-X

Library of Congress Catalog Card No.: 96-90244

0 9 8 7 6 5 4 3 2

# *Wait for True Love*

10/24/21 - 9/29/08

# Chapter 1

Ashley was a girl from a family of four children. She lived on a farm with her dad and mom along with her three sisters. The children were all taught to work hard. There were ten cows to milk by hand early mornings and evenings. Ashley attended grade school in a one-room school with all eight grades. She hated school. She would rather stay at home and help with the chores and help her dad doing "farm work." Her sisters all liked school and were glad they could attend school, rather than stay at home and do manual labor.

Each morning at the breakfast table, dad would say something like, "I have to mow alfalfa and load it in the wagon to put in the hay loft in the barn. Who wants to stay home from school to help with that?" Each older child would look at Ashley and know Ashley would volunteer, and so she did. She would say, "I'll stay home to help you, Dad."

Her dad was pleased. When he was a boy he'd hated school, too, so he knew how Ashley felt and didn't mind her missing school. Ashley finished and graduated from grade school and started to attend high school, which she disliked, all but literature. She was good at that and liked her teacher, which made it more likeable. Before this, however, in spite of helping with the farm work, she had been a fair student in grade school.

One day in her fourth grade year they started a spelling

bee with the fourth grade to the eighth grade. Ashley spelled all eight grades down. She was a terrific speller. She couldn't wait to get home and tell her folks she'd spelled all eight grades down. Her folks were very proud of her. Ashley remembered to this day what she'd accomplished. Later on, in high school, she rode on a yellow schoolbus to school, as it was quite a distance from home. At the closing of each day, she was always afraid she would get on the wrong bus, and this frightened her. She found out in time to get off and enter her own bus. She had that fear each day that she would get on the wrong bus. Ashley cheated a lot, and would look at other students' papers whenever they had a test. She even asked one boy to do her "homework" for the next day, that is. He liked Ashley and so did it for her. She finished the sophomore year and quit school completely. Her dad said, "If you can find a job outside of home, you won't have to finish school." This made her very happy. She knew of a family where the wife was expecting a baby and already had three children. So she called up this family and asked the woman if she could use a hired girl. The lady was ecstatic and said, "Sure, I need someone to help me when the baby comes." This woman had heard all about Ashley and her sisters, what hard workers they were at home. Ashley was paid three dollars a week.

She worked hard and was liked very much in the home. The baby came, and after working there three months, Ashley applied for a waitress job in her home town of Abilene, Kansas. Ashley was hired and was liked so well by her employers that she became the head waitress. She would get up at five o'clock and would unlock the restaurant and get coffee made at once, as they opened at six-thirty. Ashley rented a room in town, and had a mile to walk each morning and night to her room, but she was energetic and a hard worker.

There were three sisters who owned the restaurant, and when a famous doctor and his wife would come in late, quite often they would ask Ashley to stay and wait on them and let the other waitresses go to their room or home, wherever they stayed. Ashley would stay until ten to eleven o'clock to serve the doctor and his wife, as they sat there for a long time and just visited. The doctor would leave a fifty-cent tip for her, which was very good money at that time. After they left, the sisters whom she worked for would either drive Ashley to her room or take her to a movie and pay her way. This made Ashley happy as she loved movies, and it was very dark to walk to her room at that time of night.

Ashley was getting very interested in boys during this time. She had begun dating when she was twelve and had had a good "bringing up," and acted straight and well behaved. When her date would start to "get fresh" with her, Ashley would "at once" put a stop to it and say, "No!" Each boy she went with seemed to honor this and kept asking for another date. Ashley accepted. By the way, her dad had told each of the girls that if ever any one of them got pregnant before being married, they would have to leave home, and he meant what he said. This attitude kept each one, especially Ashley careful; in fact, on each date she had, she played "hard to get." In those days, they didn't understand about sex; how untrue that is today. One time Ashley came home and told her mom she was pregnant. Her mom looked aghast and said, "Ashley, what did you do?" and she said, "I kissed him." Her mom said, "Is that all?" and she said "Yes." Her mom said, "No, you're not pregnant." Ashley was relieved. In those days parents didn't explain about sex. Their children just knew to behave.

One time in grade school, her cousin was sitting behind her and whispered to Ashley, "You have blood on your dress." Ashley was so scared and they went to the outside toilet and her cousin informed her that she had her "period." The teacher was a very nice man and was married. Ashley said to her cousin, "I can't go into the schoolroom with blood on my dress. What shall I do?" Her cousin said, "Go home and I'll tell the teacher you went home because you were sick." A true statement really! Ashley had to walk one and one-half miles to her home, and her dad was in the field working, driving a tractor. When he saw her coming up the lane, he thought she'd been bad and had been sent home from school, so he started for home at once. When he got home, he jumped off the tractor and started for the house. Well, her mom had seen the blood on Ashley's dress and knew at once she had her period, so she quickly went to her husband and told him, "No, don't go in the house. I'll explain." That evening her dad was so nice to her, very, exceptionally nice. He felt sorry for her because she hadn't been told about "having periods." More than you can say for the teenagers today. Ashley's mom still didn't tell her about sex, only to say that it would happen once a month, her period, that is. That's all her mom ever told her. Later, she found out her three other sisters were told about periods, and I don't know how much more, but that's beside the point.

Ashley was interested in Chris Engle, whom she met at a church social. She also had her eyes on James Bennington. She liked him a lot. She was dating Chris and she liked him, but she thought about James, too, and wished he would ask her for a date. The two teenage boys didn't know each other. One day by chance James came into the restaurant and sat at the table Ashley was waiting on. They talked some and before he left, he asked her if she cared to go to a movie that was playing and was rated high. She was excited and accepted.

The date went well, and after the movie, they went to a drugstore for ice cream. They talked a lot and Ashley found out he was a regular Sunday school attender at a local church in town. She heard from Chris again and they had another date. She didn't mention to him about James, but somehow or other, he heard she was seeing James. Both of the teenagers were "clean cut" boys and both had attended church since they were small boys. She liked that a lot. She liked them both and continued dating Chris and James.

In the meantime, Ashley went to a church convention in Ohio. She went with her folks. She was pleased to see several boys whom she wished she could meet. During lunch hour she was sitting across the table from one of the fellows she had her eyes on. They each introduced themselves to each other and both seemed to "hit it off" with one another. His name was Jack Riley. They saw quite a lot of each other while at the convention. When the convention was over, they both agreed to correspond, which they did.

After returning home from Ohio, Ashley went back to work as a waitress. In the meantime, Jim, which is short for James, was making plans to go to medical school in Texas. He had been leaning toward being a doctor for a long time. Ashley knew she would miss him, but they decided to continue writing after he was gone. Chris heard Ashley was home from the convention and called her up and they set a date to meet the following Friday evening, as he had something he wanted to discuss with her.

The evening came and they were both delighted to see each other. Two weeks was a long time to be separated, as they had become very good friends. They gave each other a long "hello kiss." Chris brought up the news almost immediately. He was going to Texas to join the navy and become a navy pilot. This was a big shock for Ashley; she knew she would miss him very much, but she was glad for him. The two agreed to correspond however. Before saying good-bye to her on their date, Chris told Ashley that he already had fallen in love with her. She said she thought she loved him, too. So one day before he left for Texas, they agreed to get married in later years, so he took her to a jeweler's and bought her a lovely engagement ring. Ashley was excited and could hardly wait to tell her mom and dad, Clarence and Ellen Cooper, and her three sisters. They were ecstatically happy and wished her the best of everything.

Meanwhile she was still corresponding with Jack Riley, whom she had met at the church convention in Ohio. Ashley liked all three but she was engaged to Chris. Still, she continued to correspond with all three.

Ashley would get weekends off from her waitress job. One weekend she and her dad had a heart-to-heart talk. She was very close to her dad, but not too close to her mom. I guess that is why her mom had never told her about getting her period or anything else about sex. Her three sisters, who were older than she, were not very close either. Ashley was the youngest. Her sisters were all dating, but not serious with anyone. Her sisters' names were Mary, Samantha, and Janet. Janet was the next in age to Ashley. They seemed to be closest; at least they could communicate. She could "open up" to Janet more. They were one year apart, which is probably why they had more in common than Mary or Samantha.

Her dad told her to know what she was doing, and she had better "break off" with Jim and Jack. She liked them, so she just continued corresponding with them, although she was wearing Chris's engagement ring. She had not told Jim and Jack she was engaged to Chris and that he was in

Texas in the Navy. One day, while Ashley was at home, Chris called and said he was on leave from the navy for a week and was coming to Abilene to see her. She was thrilled, and she went to the restaurant and told the sisters whom she worked for that she would like off for a week and why. They didn't want to lose her, so they said, "Sure, we'll manage somehow." She was thrilled, and left to go home to get ready to entertain Chris. Ashley's mom and dad were excited and wanted to meet him. Mom and Dad Cooper lived on a 360-acre farm, which they owned. Since the summer crops were all in, and planting for the winter months was yet to be done, they had a breather, so they could properly entertain Chris.

Ashley's sisters, Mary and Samantha, were getting enthusiastic about entering college in the fall. Janet was still at home not knowing just yet what she wanted to do or be. One day Ashley went outside to bring the mail in which the mail carrier had just left and there was a letter from Jim, who was in Kentucky in medical school. She rapidly tore open the letter and read it slowly and near to the end, he said he was very busy, liked medical school a lot, but he missed her and really cared a lot for her. He didn't know when his first break from school would be, so he asked her if she could come out to Kentucky to visit him for a few days, and that she could stay with his "buddy's" girlfriend while she was there. Ashley was excited but in shock. She knew she couldn't get serious with two guys and continue to correspond with Jack who lived in Ohio where they had met at convention, some time ago. She had to discontinue corresponding with Jack, as she believed she cared for him the least, and anyway she was committed to Chris and was wearing his engagement ring. She wanted it settled one way or the other before Chris got there, as this was bothering her a lot.

Well, at a minute's notice, she sat down and wrote Jack a letter rather hastily. She told him she was involved with a navy pilot and would have to break-up corresponding with him, not mentioning Jim at all. She asked her dad if she could borrow the car to take a letter to the post office, which seemed important to her to mail it at once. "Of course," her dad said. "Sure, honey, but be careful." This meant a lot to Ashley. Now, it was down to two, Jim in medical school and Chris, her fiancé. Well, she had to write to Jim yet and answer his invitation to visit him soon, or sometime in the near future. However, she left that on "hold" for a few days or so. She was concentrating on Chris's arrival from the Navy and being his fiancée. The Coopers met Chris at the bus depot, as he didn't have the money to fly, and he didn't make that much money in Navy school. He was training to be a helicopter pilot. Mom and Dad Cooper waited until Ashley and Chris had their "hello" kiss and chatted awhile. Then he was introduced to Mom and Dad Cooper. Ashley told Chris to just call them "Mom and Dad," as that would make it easier, and less complicated while he was there, so that is what he did. The four went to the Cooper farm and Chris and Ashley had access to the family car. Anyway her Dad promised to buy Ashley a car of her own. Well, the next day her Dad thought it was time he gave her a car now as that would make it more simpler to show Chris around, and to do and go wherever they liked. This he did. Mary and Samantha already had second-hand cars, which were late models and Janet was using her folks' car when she needed it, but was thinking about owning her own in the near future.

    Ashley and Chris were so much in love and had a great time going and seeing places of interest and just being alone, kissing and hugging and enjoying each other's presence. The days came and went; it was nearly time for Chris to return to Texas where he was stationed. Bus travel was rather slow so Dad Cooper bought Chris a plane ticket so he could fly back after staying over several more days. But all good things must come to an end, for now it was the day he was leaving. Ashley drove Chris to Wichita to catch the plane. Janet went with them, so Ashley would have company returning home. It was quiet riding home. Ashley was missing Chris already, but she knew she had to give Jim an answer to his invitation to go visit him in medical school.

When they arrived home, there was a message for her from her mom. She was to call Jim immediately and he had given her his telephone number. Ashley waited until the evening to call Jim, as she figured he would be in school throughout the day. She wondered all day what was so important. Could it be he was breaking up with her, but no, she was sure it wasn't that, as he had just written her concerning coming to visit him. But what was it? Well, she would soon know as it was nearly seven o'clock and she would soon have the answer, so she called him, hoping he was in his room awaiting the call. Sure enough, he was there, and with delight answered the phone. Jim told her he was going to Kansas University at Lawrence, Kansas, for part of his medical training and then they could see and visit each other, as it was not too far from Abilene. Ashley was excited to say the least and told Jim she was ecstatically happy. It would be another month before he would arrive at K.U. They talked more in length and then they both "hung up."

Ashley was getting conscience stricken then, and thought about Chris, and the engagement ring on her finger. She hastily told her mom and dad and sisters. They all at once thought about her fiancé, Chris, and how she was going to handle it. Being very close to her dad, rather than her mom, she wanted some advice from him. He said jokingly, "Just don't get your letters mixed up and in the wrong envelopes." Then he apologized and said he was sorry, it was nothing to joke about. He mentioned she could break up with Jim and tell him she was already engaged to a Navy pilot in Dallas-Fort Worth. That was the truthful way out, but she knew he would be in Kansas in around a month and wanted to see him very much, and that Chris was miles away and it would help fill her time being with Jim occasionally.

There was a letter in the mail that day from Ohio. It was from Jack. She tore it open at once, anxious to know how he took her breaking up with him. She read fast until she came to the important part. He said it was a great shock to him and he had thought she liked him very much. He already felt he was falling in love with her, but wanted to be sure that was what she wanted, and if they still could see each other just as friends, at least. The letter went on to say he was busy in the bank and was promoted to a higher position and that he felt in a few years, or even less, he could support a wife. Ashley's heart beat rapidly and she was excited, then, too. She didn't know how long Chris and she would have to wait to get married. She folded up the letter and tucked it in one of her dresser drawers. At that point she thought, she would just let the letter ride, and not answer his letter just yet, anyway. After all, she did "break up" the correspondence.

Getting back to her work as a waitress, she quit that job, as there was not likely any promotion in it ever. She decided to stay home for a while and help on the farm or whatever there was to do; anyway, she needed time alone to think and weigh the consequences. Mary and Samantha were packing for college. Janet was undecided what she wanted to do. College was out, she thought. She didn't feel like she wanted to go to college, not now, anyway. Ashley couldn't go to college and she had never even finished high school. She had a friend who went to California and was working as a maid in rich peoples' homes, and who never finished high school, either. She thought that would be interesting, and something she wouldn't need a diploma for. She would talk it over with her dad. He was a good listener and he would probably say that would be good, it would get her away from having to see Jim who would soon be moving to Kansas for medical school, at K.U., Lawrence, Kansas.

Ashley was a blonde with natural wavy hair, a very pretty girl. Her three sisters were very attractive. They had dates off and on with boys in and around Abilene, but none of them were serious, and didn't have the problem, if you can call it a problem, Ashley did. In some respects they were jealous of her. Chris had black curly hair, and was very handsome, as were Jim and Jack as well, but she didn't have to worry about Jack, as she did break up corresponding with him. Jim would soon be coming to Lawrence, Kansas, and time was going by swiftly. Ashley's mom and three sisters went last minute shopping before Mary and Samantha were to be leaving for college. Ashley stayed at home, as she knew her dad was outside working at something around the farm. She went outside to find him and found him in the barn filling troughs with hay for the cattle's evening feeding. When he saw Ashley, he put down his hay rake and knew Ashley had something on her mind. He asked her if she wanted to talk. She immediately said, "Yes, Dad, there is something troubling me and I need some answers."

So they talked for what seemed like an hour. Her dad said the decision was hers, but he did give some advice. It all amounted to, you can't have two men seriously involved and not hurt one or the other. They both decided she would at least see Jim when he comes, and go from there. That didn't settle much, but it was a beginning. She learned about God in Sunday school and asked Him to guide and direct her, in the right thing to do, and when she said "the right thing," in her heart she knew from wrong, but she did wish she knew their pastor better. She would have liked to have some counseling. Her mom and dad had taken the four girls to Sunday school, but for some reason she just stopped going after a while.

Now an idea popped into Ashley's mind. *Tomorrow is Sunday. I'm going to church.* Her parents and sisters were astonished when Ashley entered the dining room all dressed up. Before they had a chance to question her, she said, "I'm going to church; anyone want to go with me?" They all gave a little shrug, as if to say "no." She was glad in a way, as she thought she might get to say "hello" to the pastor after the sermon was over and make herself known. She didn't hear too much of the sermon, because she had a lot on her mind, but what she did hear, she liked, feeling he would be easy to talk to.

Pastor Monroe Smucker clasped her hand as she was going out the door and said, "I don't believe I know you, but it sure was nice to have you in church today." She then told him she used to attend regularly when she was a small girl, but her parents for one reason or another had just stopped coming. That's about all the time either had to talk, as a line of people had formed behind her to greet the pastor. However, he invited her to come back and she promised she would. On the way home from church, she knew in her heart she would see him again, but also she knew what she had to do. She reasoned within herself, *I can't keep dating Jim when I'm engaged to Chris,* but she had deep feelings for Jim, too. She was again glad she had broken up with Jack and knew too, she liked him a lot. She then said out loud to herself, "What a mess you got yourself into, Ashley," but she wanted to hear it from the pastor.

The next day, Monday, she called the pastor, and his wife gave her the church number and told her to call him there, as he was in his study, but that it would be all right to call him. So she did. Pastor Smucker was surprised to hear her voice as he remembered her name from yesterday. She asked him if he had a few minutes for her, as there was something urgent she wanted to talk to him about. He immediately replied he would be glad to, but he would have to check his schedule for the week, and if she would give him her number, he would call her and let her know when he could give her an appointment. She gladly did this, and thanked him and hung up. Already she felt relieved. She felt if he knew the situation, she could better know how to handle the problem, as she knew right from wrong, but wanted the pastor to "back her up" so to speak.

Then Ashley thought about having gone to church since she was a girl. She had heard about the convention and just all of a sudden went. She was talking aloud to herself, "and that's where I met Jack, and he is a regular church-goer. Was I supposed to go and meet him? Now I am getting confused, but wait a minute, I have broken off with him." Oh, she was glad she was seeing the pastor, Rev. Smucker. About that time, the telephone rang, and it was the pastor calling. He told her his week was filled up, but he had all afternoon if she could work it in then. Ashley was delighted and said, "That is fine, what time?" He said, "Come over now if it's convenient." She thanked him and hurriedly went out to her car. Her heart was beating rapidly. *Now just how do I start this?* she was thinking. She arrived at the church, met him, and he took her to his study. They visited a little and then he said, "Now Ashley, what seems to be troubling you?" and she began abruptly and told him first about Jack and having broken off their correspondence, then about Jim and her fiancé Chris. He said, "I notice you're wearing an engagement ring."

She said, "That's the problem, pastor. I'm wondering if I should be wearing it." Ashley told about his visit to their home and seeing her, just a few weeks ago, and how in love they both were, but that Jim was coming back to Lawrence, Kansas, to take up medical study there and she had promised him she would see him.

The discussion went on, and finally Pastor Smucker said, "I think now is the time to have a word of prayer. God always listens and works things out better than you or I could, if you just trust 'Him.' " When the prayer was over, Ashley felt so calm and serene and thanked the pastor and left. On the way home, Ashley felt so calm and just knew seeing Jim would work out all right.

Mary and Samantha were in college now at K-State in Manhattan, Kansas. They were rooming there and could have driven back and forth to their home and school, but they wanted to get the thrill of "dorm" life, and of course their dad could certainly afford it. Their dad was thinking of selling all his cattle off and not having the bother of milking them each morning and evening, having only to farm the ground and raise wheat and oats. That alone would be enough to keep him busy, with his not being able to count on Ashley, as she had a life of her own now. So, this is what he did. He sold all the cattle and livestock, and four horses. He felt free and thought perhaps Ellen, his wife and he could do some much-wanted traveling. The girls were all glad for them.

Janet was still at home and was dating some with local boys. Ashley told Janet she should be somewhere or doing something where men were available. Janet confessed she was getting more bored the older she was getting, but still didn't want to go to college, not now anyway. Ashley reminded her what her friend was doing, in California working in the homes of rich people, as a maid, and from all her letters she apparently was enjoying it very much. Janet said she would think about it and maybe that was what she should do. Ashley was still at home after giving up her waitress job and had some things to get straightened out before she could make any decisions. Jim would be at K.U. in two weeks, and Ashley was eagerly awaiting that, and hoping to get things settled about dating him, especially when she was engaged to Chris. Ashley wrote Chris once a week and he looked forward to her letters, being so far from home, and lonely at times. When she wrote to Chris, she would always end her letters, "your future wife and all my love, Ashley." It was time she heard from Chris again.

Maybe today she would get a letter in the mail, and that's just what happened. Janet brought the mail in and waved a letter in front of Ashley. Sure enough, it was from Chris. She hurriedly opened the letter and went to her room upstairs to read it, as she liked being alone; she could concentrate better. The letter made her excited. He told her how much he missed her and how much he loved her, and longed for the day they would be husband and wife. Again Ashley thought about Jim's soon arrival. She went to church regularly now and somehow she felt good about it. It helped her to have faith in herself and that God would help her do the right thing.

# Chapter 2

There was Jack too, whom she had met at a church convention. Since she started to go to church regularly and she felt good after having gone, she, all of a sudden, wished in a way she had not quit corresponding with Jack. All of a sudden, she missed him and even thought about writing him and telling him it was a mistake because she still felt a lot for him. Then she remembered what Pastor Monroe said to her. *Oh dear,* she thought, *why can't you love them all?* Of course that would be out of the question. She was in deep thought when the telephone rang. It was Jim calling her from K.U. and telling her of his arrival at Lawrence, Kansas. She was shaking when she was talking to him, as she knew soon she would have to make a decision. It was Tuesday, and Jim wanted to drive to her home over the weekend, and would that suit her? He said he was looking forward to this for a long time it seemed. Ashley "stalled" a minute, then said, "Why don't you come Saturday afternoon and spend the night here as we have an empty room and could accommodate you, and leave on Sunday afternoon?"

He said, "That sounds fine to me, but could you give me the directions as how to get there?" She said she was not very good at giving directions but to give her his number and she would have her dad call him Tuesday evening and give directions. Jim said he would be in his room around seven o'clock, to call him then. They wished each other good-bye over the phone and hung up.

All of a sudden, Ashley looked at her finger. The ring. "He'll see my engagement ring." Her face felt hot. She was shaking, but not for long, because she remembered what she heard Pastor Smucker say in church last Sunday morning. She was still, very still. Her faith took hold, and peace came into her being. She'd let him see it on her finger, and then he'd know. She felt that was a cowardly way out, but she thought that was the way she would handle it.

The big day arrived. It was in the afternoon when she saw a sleek white car pull up in the driveway. She ran out to meet him. He jumped out of the car and they kissed and embraced each other. Ashley thought, *He looks so handsome.*

They held hands as they walked into the house. Her mom was in the kitchen preparing dinner, but she made herself known, and welcomed him. They made "small talk," and then she excused herself and went out to the kitchen. Ashley took Jim into the den where the whole family liked to "hang out." They were seated and both started talking at once. They each gave a little laugh, then Jim spoke, and said, "It's as though we both want to talk at once. You go on, Ashley, tell me what you've been up to."

She then said, "I'm going to church regularly Sunday mornings and I love it."

Jim said, "Oh, sounds interesting," then it happened. They were holding hands and he felt something, and he looked and saw the ring. He was stunned, then said, "Is there something you want to tell me, maybe about church or something?"

She blurted out like a "bolt from the blue," "I'm engaged to a fellow, Chris Engle. He's in Texas in the Navy.

He's learning to fly a helicopter. I wanted to tell you sooner, but I still had feelings for you and, well, I just put it off."

He looked in her eyes, and noticed a "tear," and said, "It's serious, isn't it?"

Then she told him, "Yes, it is. I love him a lot, but I think I'm in love with two other fellows too." Then she told him about Jack who lived in Ohio and got a big promotion in the bank there.

Jim asked, "Who is the other fellow?"

Ashley looked startled and said, "Silly, you, of course." He pulled her over to him and she lay in his arms.

It seemed minutes before either talked and then Jim said, "Thanks, Ashley, for being so honest." She told him of her counseling with her pastor and how he told her it wasn't fair to the others to get involved with any other than the one she's engaged to. If she didn't quote it , that's what it amounted to. Jim asked, "Ashley, do you believe that?"

Ashley said, "Yes, I had 'good' bringing up from my parents, but it is so hard." Then she said to Jim, "I already broke up with Jack. We stopped corresponding," but added, "he still says he loves me." Ashley excused herself and went to the kitchen to check on dinner, and when they would eat.

Her mom said, "Your dad isn't back yet, but when he gets here, we'll eat." Ashley went back into the den and told Jim they would have time to go for a walk because her dad wasn't home yet, and they could go for a short walk if he cared to. He agreed, anything but to face the reality that the one he loved was engaged to another fellow. They had a long lane, and they walked holding hands. The ring that Jim felt was evidence of the truth, that Ashley belonged to some other fellow. They stood still a minute and looked into each other's eyes.

Then Jim spoke and said, "Can we still be good friends, and see each other once in a while?"

Ashley was delighted and said, "Do you really mean that?"

Jim said, "Yes, we don't need to let our weekend be spoiled." They gave each other a squeeze of their hands and then saw Ashley's dad coming home, so they abruptly walked back to the house for dinner. Clarence Cooper welcomed Jim to their home and told him he would like to show him around the farm after dinner, while the dishes were being done. Jim agreed. Dad Cooper took pride in his farm and "kept it up" well, as did Mom Cooper in caring for her house.

At the dinner table, Dad Cooper and Jim did most of the talking. Dad noticed he and Ashley were unreasonably quiet. Then he thought of the ring on Ashley's finger, and he knew Jim had noticed it and that's why there was little talking between the two. Dinner was over and it took little time to do the dishes, as they had a dishwasher. While they were putting away the dishes and tidying up, Mom asked Ashley about the ring and if Jim had noticed it. She nodded her head and said, "We agreed to just be friends and see each other occasionally."

Mom said, "Do you think that is wise, Ashley?"

Ashley said, "Jim is very busy with medical school, so he won't be around very much," and then she wondered, *Will he be around at all?*

Dad and Jim both came into the house after they saw the farm. Jim was impressed greatly! Jim and Ashley were alone now and Jim said, "Why don't we go for a drive and see this country of yours, which used to be mine before my folks moved to Florida." Ashley agreed that would be nice.

After a nice drive, but "too little" talk, they arrived home. Sunday morning came and Ashley asked Jim if he would like to go to church with her, and he said, "That would be nice. Sure I'll go."

After church, many people wanted to meet the young man who was with Ashley. She introduced him as "a very good friend." That seemed the logical thing to say, and it seemed to suffice. Ashley and Jim went to the Coopers' home for lunch.

Then Jim said, "I'd better be going." And he thanked the Coopers for their kind hospitality. Ashley walked out to the car with Jim, and he gave her a good-bye kiss and said, "For old times sake." Ashley stood still and watched Jim driving off and didn't take her eyes off the car until it was out of sight. She was relived that was over. She was startled as the telephone rang.

It was the hospital in Texas. The doctor told Ashley that Chris was in the hospital, he had gotten hurt in training. She asked the name of the hospital and said she would be leaving as soon as she got a plane ticket. Then she prayed, "Dear God, don't let him be seriously hurt," and to spare him until she got there at least. Her dad came into the house and asked her what was going on as she was shaking. She told her dad and asked him to call the airport and get a ticket for that same day. He wasn't quite so fortunate, as there was nothing going out that day, but he left his number in case there was a cancellation. Ashley was already upstairs packing a light suitcase with a minimum of clothes. The telephone rang and Dad Cooper answered it. She was fortunate and could leave that same night and fly at night. Dad said, "Save it, we'll take it."

They left early for the airport. Ashley breathed a prayer as they were driving to the airport and asked God to let Chris be well enough so he would know that she was there with him. The plane was on time and she was thankful. Her dad gave her a big hug and said, "I'll pray." This was unusual to Ashley, but she knew he would do just that. Ashley asked the stewardess if she had a relaxer pill or something to calm her down. She said she couldn't do that, but she would make her a cup of hot tea. Ashley thanked her and said that would be fine. She asked the stewardess if the plane would get there on time, and she assured her, "So far it is on time." Ashley sipped her tea slowly and then felt more relaxed already. She was praying to God, and thinking of her pastor telling her on Sunday when he was preaching to have faith in God. This reassured her greatly.

Finally, after what seemed too long, the plane came in for a landing. It was slow getting off the plane, but she found herself going up to the information booth. The girl who was there told her to go outside as there were taxi cabs waiting. This she did and found one. The cab driver got out and opened the door for her and took her small bag and placed it down beside her. Ashley asked how far it was to the hospital. He said, approximately twenty miles, but her dad had given her more than enough money for her expenses, so she told the driver to drive her there, and hurry. He was accommodating and she knew he was going faster than the speed limit, but that was all right. He had a good excuse if any cop stopped them. She saw the hospital and was relieved to be there. She paid the cab driver a nice fare and thanked him. She went inside and asked someone if she could see Navy Pilot Chris Engle. The nurse asked if she was related to him and she said, "I'm his fiancée."

She said, "Oh, he'll be glad to see you. Come this way." The nurse opened the door and Ashley "tiptoed" in the room. Chris had his eyes closed. She went over to the bed and leaned over to kiss him when he opened his eyes. He was shocked, but thrilled to see her to say the least. Then Ashley gave him a real kiss. He wanted to know how she knew, and before she answered, he remembered he asked the doctor if he would call her up and let her know. They looked fondly at each other. Then Ashley asked how it happened and if it was serious. She realized she shouldn't have asked him that and was upset with herself.

Chris said, "Oh, I'll be fine. I was down in X-ray all day yesterday, and also had a 'cat scan.'" He said he had a severe concussion and several broken ribs and a wound in his forehead, which was covered with a large patch. He said he'd have to have plastic surgery on his head when it healed. He said he was fortunate, the other pilot wasn't so fortunate. "Oh no," he added, "he'll be all right, but he had a number of broken bones, plus a bad head concussion."

Ashley said, "Maybe I should leave. Are you sure you should be talking?"

Chris said, "You are the best medicine I could have, but you're right, I should lie very still and guess I shouldn't be talking so much." So Ashley sat on a chair beside his bed and held his hand.

Then the nurse came in and said, "Miss, you should leave soon. He has got to rest."

Ashley said, "Sure, I'll leave now, but Chris, I'll be back tomorrow."

As she started towards the door Chris said, "Ashley honey, thanks for coming." She went back and gave him a good-bye kiss and left. When she left the room, she went up to the nurses' station and told them she was from Kansas and had flown out because of Chris's accident, and asked if they knew where she could get a room for a few days. One nurse was due to leave for the day and sent her to the waiting room and told her she'd try and help her in a few minutes when she was off work, if she wanted to wait. Ashley agreed, found her way to the waiting room, and waited. Ashley thought, *He looks so helpless. I'm used to a strong, handsome guy with black curly hair. He doesn't seem to me, as the same person.* Then she thought, *What am I thinking? He'll soon be up and around, he'll be the same. He's been hurt by an accident, just give him time.* The nurse appeared. She said, "Oh, here you are. I might have something if you're interested." Ashley listened. It just happened that her roommate was on two weeks leave and by the way, she said, "My name is Marie. You could room with me until you find something."

Ashley was delighted, and she was tired, too, having traveled all night with very little sleep, and she was hungry, too. So she said to Marie, "I'll go pick up my bag and I'll meet you at the front entrance if that's all right?"

Marie said, "That's fine. I'll be there."

Ashley got her bag and followed Marie out to her car. She was glad she didn't have to look right away for a room, as she suddenly felt as if she could drop. Marie glanced at her while driving and said, "Are you all right?" Ashley told her about having traveled all night with very little sleep and not having anything to eat on the plane as she felt she couldn't eat then because of fearing what she might find when she got to the hospital. So they stopped at a place where Marie quite often stopped for breakfast on her way to work and received a menu from the waitress. Ashley felt better after she had eaten and told Marie she must call her mom and dad to let them know she was all right and inform them about Chris, too. So when they arrived at Marie's room, she at once put a call to her folks' place. Dad answered and was relieved to hear her voice and all the news about Chris and where she was fortunate to be staying. They were happy to hear that, as they were wondering all about the trip, her whereabouts, and especially that Chris was all right, with the proper rest and so on. Ashley said good-bye to her Dad and hung up.

Marie told Ashley, "You should have seen Chris when

they brought him in on a stretcher with blood from his forehead and running down his face." It was she who had cleaned him up just before the doctor came to examine him. She told Ashley, "You're fortunate. As they come in here to the Navy hospital some come in who are not so fortunate." Then she assured her the doctor said he was going to be fine after two or three days and then could even leave the hospital. Ashley was thrilled to hear that. She told herself she should have been more thankful than feeling sorry for herself. Then the word "faith" in God came into her mind, what Pastor Monroe spoke about from the pulpit so often.

We'll put Ashley, Chris and Marie on hold for a while, and go back to what her mom and dad and her sisters Mary and Samantha were up to. Ashley's sisters were at home on a college break she found out from her dad, as Marie had given them her telephone number to call whenever they liked. Ashley was pleased about that, as she all of a sudden felt "so alone" and out of touch. Ashley wasn't used to being alone and caring for herself a lot, as she always had Dad and Mom to look out for her. Now she was facing reality, and realized she was a big girl now and engaged to be married. When she came to that conclusion, she felt so much better, and breathed a sigh of relief, even so much so that Marie noticed. Ashley apologized and said she was thinking, as she had a lot on her mind.

Then the telephone rang and it was for Ashley again. It was her mom this time. She told Ashley that Janet was in California looking for a job as a maid in rich people's homes and that Ashley's friend was going to help find her a job. Ashley asked when did all this happen and why? Her Mom said that Janet was just bored with all three sisters gone and she wanted something better and worthwhile to do, and that her dad sent money with her to look for a car, preferably a secondhand one so she could get around better, and come and go as she pleased.

Then Ashley said, "Oh, Mom, I wish I were with her," and her mom thought this strange as she was with her fiancé, Chris. Then Ashley said, "Oh, never mind, Mom, I'm all right. I need sleep badly." She told her to call again and hung up after a good-bye. Marie thought Ashley looked tired and asked her if she wanted to take a rest, adding that her roommate's bed had just been "made up." She thanked her and admitted that sounded so good. "I just need some sleep, then I'll be all right." She actually fell asleep and slept for three hours, then she was surprised how good she felt and was ready for the next day when she would see Chris again. Now she wished she had her car there in Texas. She hated to rely on cabs, but she would just get along as best she could.

Marie fixed a quick, but nice lunch, and then they talked. Marie wasn't seeing anyone steady, "run of the mill" fellows. She thought Ashley had an interesting and exciting life. She admired the ring on her finger, the engagement ring Chris had given her. Ashley admitted maybe she was too hasty in becoming engaged. Well, tomorrow she would see Chris again and after a good night sleep, it would "all be well." Morning came and Marie had to go to work early. Ashley rode along with her and waited in the waiting room until Chris was "made up" for the day. It was nine o'clock and she went to the desk and inquired about visiting hours. Knowing it was her fiancé, and she had come clear from Kansas to see him, they allowed her to go in his room as he was "made up" for the day. They told her the doctor was coming in to see him in a while. So Ashley walked up to the door and knocked, and opened it slowly. There she found Chris up and sitting in a chair. Ashley was overwhelmed and surprised to see him looking so good. She went up to him and gave him a big good morning kiss. He returned the favor. She asked him how long he would be in the hospital. Chris said he would know this morning when he had a visit from his doctor. He said he felt unusually good, except for his broken ribs. And a bit dizzy from the concussion. Ashley said not to get too tired, and if her visiting was making him tired, to please let her know and she would leave. He nodded his head as if to say okay.

The doctor came in and Ashley met him, then stepped out of the room. The doctor checked Chris over and told him he could leave the hospital the next day, but would have to take it easy for several weeks, and not go back to work for a month, because of his severe concussion. He would have to see a doctor wherever he was for a check-up occasionally. He met Ashley outside the room and said, "You're his fiance," and she said yes. He told her, "Chris is coming along fine" and a repeat of what he told Chris. Then Ashley asked if he could go home for a visit until he was ready to go back to work.

She added, "I'd go with him on the plane and look after him," and that he lived in Kansas where she was from and could rest up at his folks' place.

The doctor agreed, and said, "That sounds like a good idea." Then he said to Ashley, "Does he know how fortunate he is to have you and a very beautiful girl at that?" Ashley smiled, and thanked him.

She went back in Chris's room and gave him the news. He was delighted, but said, "First, I'll have to inform my Navy officers of my plans and whereabouts." So Ashley said, "Of course." He said he would have to go to his Navy headquarters and pack a few things, that he looked awful as he hadn't shaved since the accident.

The next morning Ashley called her folks and let them

know about his coming home for a month's furlough to recuperate; then she told them that she was coming with him to care for him on the trip. They were pleased. Ashley made reservations for a plane flight for two. She went and told Chris the plans. When it was time to go to the airport, she called a cab and asked Chris where she would meet him so they could both go together to the airport. This they did and before long, they were on the plane flying back to Kansas. She got them both "first class" tickets, as she thought that would be more comfortable for Chris. They held hands until lunch was served. She wanted to hug him but couldn't because of his broken ribs. She gave him a "peck" on the cheek occasionally. They had an hour layover in Chicago. She had the stewardess call ahead and to have a wheelchair ready. She thought, *This isn't like me to make all the arrangements. I was the one who was waited on all the time by Dad and Mom.* It gave her a "grown-up" feeling, and she liked it.

Things went well in Chicago. It was time for the plane to leave in thirty minutes, and she got an "aid" to put Chris on the plane early because of his wheelchair. Of course Ashley was there with him. They were settled in their seats and it was soon time for the plane to take off, as it did in minutes.

Ashley breathed a sigh of relief. Chris had always been the strong one who did everything for himself and others, too, but he would be well again and return to his usual self, she had been assured. It was an easy flight. The stewardess took good care of them both and then they were told to prepare for landing. At the airport Ashley saw her folks and Chris's folks there awaiting the arrival. Ashley and Chris gave each other a long kiss and they went their separate ways.

When in the car, she gave a big sigh of relief and her

folks wondered why. She told them she had done a lot of "growing up" since they last saw her. Then she went into detail and told them "all." Ashley missed seeing Janet and was surprised Mary and Samantha had returned to college. She would have liked to have seen them. The next day was Sunday and she felt too tired to go to church, but went anyway. She asked her folks if they would like to go with her. They gave a faint nod, as if to say no, then her dad said maybe sometime, "BABY." She hoped very much so. Clarence and Ellen Cooper felt sorry to leave Ashley to go alone. Then her dad said to her mom, "Why don't we try it? We may like it, and it has been so long and Ashley certainly has changed since she started going to church." Ashley's mom said, "Maybe next Sunday." She meant it too!

Ashley went upstairs after church to unpack her bag. Then she opened her drawer and there was Jack's letter, written after she called off corresponding. She looked at it a minute, then picked it up and read it again. He talked about his promotion and that he could support a wife. She somehow wished this could be true. She even felt like dropping him a line, but, *Well, it's time for dinner, I had better go downstairs.*

Chris was the main subject at the dinner table. Ashley said she was going to call him after the dishes were cleaned up and put away. Having a dishwasher made it easy. She did as she said she would. She called Chris and he sounded so good. She knew by his tone of voice he really did feel good. She asked when she could drive down to see him. He said, "Give me a couple more days, and I'll be my old self again." She suggested Wednesday, and he said that sounded fine. He said, "Just a minute," and he asked his mom if Ashley could come for lunch. She said, "Sure, that will be fine, and I need to get better acquainted with her." So they left it at that. Ashley would see him on Wednesday.

Ashley went upstairs again, and did a lot of thinking. She thought there wasn't much future in Chris and her becoming husband and wife very soon. He was in the Navy and the pay wasn't that great, and he would be there for who knew how long.

Then she thought about Jim down in Lawrence, Kansas, a medical student. She thought, *If I could only see him occasionally, that would be nice,* but she was wearing Chris's ring, and he knew now she was engaged to be married, so she thought, there would be no letters even. She felt like writing him that afternoon, but thought better of it.

Then Jack wandered into her mind. His last letter to her was so neat. He wanted to be friends and said he felt he could soon marry her with his promotion. She really dwelled on that! She was somewhat bored and wanted excitement, when all of a sudden she "snapped to" inside, and thought, *Why am I thinking like that? I'll see my fiancé Wednesday, and we'll see what comes out of that visit.*

In the meantime Chris was looking at the blood-stained Navy suit he took out of his "duffle bag." It was a mess since he had his accident. He had shoved it in his bag in Texas when he hurriedly packed to go back to his home in Kansas. Then he thought, *Ashley never even saw me in my uniform.* He then asked his mom if she would take it to the dry cleaners and could he have it by Wednesday when Ashley would see him in it. She said, "Of course, I'll take it in tomorrow morning or preferably by Tuesday evening." She was happy when they told her she could pick it up Tuesday evening. She thanked them and left. She too, wanted to see him in his Navy uniform.

Wednesday couldn't come soon enough for both Chris and Ashley. Chris felt better all the time and thought a month from the Navy would be too long to be out of training. *Well,* he thought, *I'll see my doctor soon and then we'll know.* He felt so good and was pleased with his progress. He was a bit "lightheaded" with his severe concussion but knew that was to be expected. Even though he felt good, he would still have to obey his doctor back in Texas and be very careful, and goodness knows, he didn't want to have a "setback." So he laid down on his bed for a while for a short rest, and thought about Wednesday and the uniform he would be wearing. The patch on his head perhaps could come off, but he better wait and see what his doctor said about that. He "so much" wanted it off, but wasn't anxious to see the wound, knowing it was bad enough for plastic surgery. He was thinking all these things and fell asleep.

At the Cooper house, the telephone rang, and Ashley answered it. It was Janet calling from California. Ashley was thrilled to hear from her and asked her to tell her everything since she arrived there. This she did. She had a job as a maid in a rich family's home and liked the people very much. They were good to her and seemed pleased with her work. Janet said, "Ashley, I need to talk to Dad, is he there?"

She told her, "He's right here. I'll put him on." They exchanged greetings, then she told him she hadn't found a car yet. She wished he was there to pick one out for her. She said her only way around to look for one was by taxi and that wasn't very practical. Her dad asked her if she needed more money and she said, "Maybe, because I have no 'trade in.' " They talked a while and then her dad told her to look around some more, and if she didn't have enough money he would wire her some. She was pleased and hung up. Then he thought, *Maybe that's too much, asking Janet to buy a car. She won't know what's a good deal or not.* He had her work number. Maybe he should call her up and tell her to just let it go for a while longer and continue to use a taxi. So that is what he did.

Janet then said, "Dad, the people I work for are very nice and maybe I could ask Mr. Sterling if he would go with me and help me buy a car." Her dad agreed, "Give it a try and let me know." They both felt in their hearts that this would be the right thing to do. It would be a very unusual thing to do, asking her employer to do this, but she wanted to give it a try.

Ashley awoke early Wednesday morning. This was the day she would see Chris again. She helped her mom do some dusting and thought, *I sure haven't been helping Mom very much with the housework. I wonder if she noticed?* Then she said, "Mom, please forgive me. I sure haven't been doing much housework. I'm sorry."

Mom said, "Oh, you've had your own problems to worry about, that's all right."

But Ashley knew in her heart she should have helped more and promised herself she was going to do something about it. *I don't even know much about cooking, and I have an engagement ring on my finger. I'm going to learn how to cook after today,* as this was the day she would see Chris. It was time to tidy herself up and leave. Then she gave her mom a big hug and said, "I'm off, I love you." Her mom wondered what brought this on, and watched Ashley as she drove out of the driveway.

Chris was all dressed up for Ashley. His mom shed a tear when she saw how handsome he looked in his uniform. She knew Ashley would be impressed. Chris looked out the window and there she was. *Even prettier than when I last saw her.* He opened the door to let her in and she stopped suddenly and a smile was on her face.

She said to Chris, "You look so handsome! I love the uniform, but I love more what's inside it." And she and

Chris both gave a little laugh. Ashley then wondered aloud where he was keeping the uniform on the way home from Texas. He explained and she said, "And I even forgot about you wearing a uniform." Then he put his hat on for show. Somehow the hat had withstood the trip in fine shape.

Chris's mom came in to welcome Ashley, and told them, "You two make a handsome couple." They both were pleased.

Chris told Ashley of his appointment to see a doctor and see when the patch on his forehead could come off, and then he said, "You may not like me when you see the wound if it's bad enough to require plastic surgery." She told him she loved the man and a wound wasn't going to interfere with that. Then they both got down to face facts about the future. Chris told Ashley he couldn't provide for her with the salary he was making in the Navy and she might get tired of waiting for him. He said, "that would break my heart if that was the case." Ashley put on a "make up" smile and told him it might not be as long as he thought, but knew in her heart that wasn't the case. then, like she was "out of it" for a moment, she was wishing they were making wedding plans.

Then when the reality hit her, she said to Chris, "Will it really be a long time?" He said the accident set him back a while as he had to miss training and he knows of a couple the man and his fiancée got married and she was a nurse, and that helped a lot with them both working. Then he added, "But, Ashley, I want to take care of my wife. I don't want to have to depend on her working." Then Ashley reminded him that she never even finished high school. She was her dad's "farm hand" instead of finishing school. She then told him she might just go to California and work as a maid in a rich family's home. She told him that's what her friend and her sister are both doing, and making good money, so she could possibly do that until they had enough money to get married. Chris didn't like that very much. Ashley could tell by the way he was looking. Then they just automatically changed the subject. Chris's mom came to the door and announced she made lunch. If they cared to, they could come and eat if they liked.

Ashley said, "I've been smelling something good. Sure, I'd like that." Chris followed. His mom announced her husband was getting home that afternoon, so she was going to wait for him, but they were to go ahead, and she excused herself. The food was delicious.

Ashley said, "Chris, we'll have to have you over some time for a meal. My mom's a good cook too." She said instead of cooking she was always out with her dad doing farm work, but that she wanted to learn how to cook better.

# Chapter 3

Chit-chat was the main topic of conversation at the table. After they had eaten, Ashley excused herself and said, "I better be on my way home," so they both got up and walked "hand in hand" to her car. They embraced ever so softly because of Chris's broken ribs and kissed hard and long, and she was off. When Ashley was driving home, she thought and felt like this afternoon was a flop. Then she hated herself for even thinking that. She reminded herself of how proud she was of Chris's joining the Navy and of how handsome he looked in his uniform. She was really proud of all the men in the service. Of how they were doing it for all of us who stayed home.

She then prayed, "Dear God, let Chris's wound on his forehead look good after they take the patch off. Don't even let him have to have plastic surgery."

Here she was, home already. The drive seemed to go so fast. Ashley's mom and dad were waiting in the living room to hear all about her trip and how Chris was doing. She told them how handsome he looked in his uniform, and how good he felt. They were pleased.

Then her mom said, "We must have Chris and his folks over for a meal some time."

Ashley said, "Do you mean that?" She told her mom she wouldn't be eating there that night, as Chris's mom fixed them a big lunch.

Then her dad said, "We were all going out to eat tonight as we have something to tell you."

Ashley said, "Oh, tell me now. I can't wait." So they told her they were getting tickets to travel around the world, and wondered if she would be all right with Janet gone and her all alone. She assured them she would be fine, and how pleased she was they were going to travel, as they had been at home working for too long. They really felt like going when she said that, and their fears were gone. Ashley went upstairs to get into something comfortable. The phone rang just before Dad and Mom Cooper were about to go out the door.

They called Ashley to come down, "Someone wants to talk to you." She hurriedly came down and to her amazement, it was Jim. He said he had all his homework finished, needed a break, and wondered if he could come up this evening and take her to a movie.

She didn't think twice, but said, "Oh yes, I'd love that. What time?" He said he was on his way then, meaning ready to leave the house. She hung up the telephone and ran upstairs to get into something nice. She felt like "dressing up" tonight. Then she thought, He's not going to take no for an answer. And she was just with her fiancé that afternoon. *Will I tell him that, or just not mention it?* Well, she would see what happens, and play it by ear. She heard the doorbell ring. She ran downstairs to let him in. She gave him a "hello" kiss, "short, but sweet." Jim was happy for that much. He asked her if she knew of anything playing that would be interesting.

She said, "I haven't heard, but why don't we just drive around and see what's playing?" He agreed to do just that.

He told Ashley she looked beautiful that night, "but then, you always do." She thanked him, and they started off for the theater. Abilene didn't have anything special playing, then Ashley suggested they drive to Salina. There were more choices there, but would it get too late for his home? He assured her it would not, so they were off. Ashley kept her distance from Jim in the car.

He noticed that, then asked, "So what have you been doing since I last saw you?" There, it was "out." She told him all about her trip to Texas to the hospital, and their trip back to Kansas, and even told him she went to see Chris that afternoon and just got home an hour ago. He was surprised at all that had happened to her and said, "Maybe you're too tired to go out?" She hastily assured him she was not. She then told him of her folks' plans to travel. He thought that was great, but said, "You have Janet," then she told him where and what Janet was doing. He then asked, "Are you comfortable staying home alone for that long a period?" She said she was not, and that Mary and Samantha would be home occasionally from college. Then they drove in silence, neither saying anything.

And then Ashley said, "We're about here." They drove around and the first theater they came to sounded interesting and clean. So they went in and the movie had just begun. The theater seemed filled, but the usher had two seats awaiting them, at last they were settled into their seats. Shortly after, Jim took Ashley's hand and held it. She was a wee bit uncomfortable, but she obliged, and even liked it. The movie was exciting and interesting, but both had other things on their minds. Jim was wishing so much Ashley was all his, but no such luck, and he wondered too, why she was so eager to go out with him tonight. Jim put his arm around her and she moved closer to him. Ashley felt an exciting chill come over her and she thought Jim must have felt the same thing, at least she hoped he did.

The movie was half over and Jim whispered to her, "Shall we leave?" She nodded "yes." They held hands on the way to the car. He put her in the driver's seat, then he got in, hoping she wouldn't move over too much. She didn't. He asked her if she would like some ice cream or something to eat. She said, "No, I'm fine." So they headed for Ashley's place. There was a silence, which seemed forever.

Then Jim spoke, "Ashley, I'm terribly in love with you."

She didn't say anything for a while, then broke the silence, "I'm falling more in love with you."

Jim said, "What are we going to do about it?"

She said, "But you know whose engagement ring I'm wearing. I really love Chris, too. How can you be in love with two at the same time?"

Jim said, "It's possible."

She said, "Surely you have to love one more than the other." And Jim said, "That's the question. Which one do you love the most?" Ashley didn't speak as she was weighing the question. She had just been with Chris this afternoon, and recalled the way Chris talked, like it would be sometime before they could be married.

Ashley was in deep thought for several minutes. *How can I break up with Chris? He's so handsome and in love with me and me with him, but I can't quit Chris now, just after his accident, and ring and all.*

Jim broke the silence. "Here we are, Ashley, at your home. You've been so quiet."

Ashley said, "I know, I was thinking about some weighty things."

Then Jim said, "Was I in them?"

She said, "Yes." Then she said, "You better go, Jim. I have to be alone and do some soul searching."

Jim said, "I respect that. May I have one big kiss before I go?" She leaned over and gave him a big hug and kissed him. He got out and he walked her to her door, and said good-night. Ashley's folks were back home and in bed, and she was relieved. She didn't want any explaining to do at that point. She ran up to her bedroom and lay on the bed and asked, "Why, God, why?" Then she burst into tears. She cried almost an hour it seemed. Then she got up and dressed for bed. Before climbing into her bed, she knelt at it and prayed, "God bless Chris, Jim, and Jack, amen!"

Ashley got up late the next morning. Her mom said, "You had a big night, so I just let you sleep."

She said, "Thanks, Mom." She wasn't in the mood for any questions just yet.

All her mom said was, "I hope you know what you're doing." Ashley was quiet. She was thinking of Chris and the doctor's report when he saw Chris. The day was a boring and long day. It was interrupted by the telephone. Ashley answered, it was Chris. He told her the patch on his forehead was removed today, and it didn't look as bad as he thought it would, but believed he'd still need plastic surgery. She asked if the doctor said he would be fit to return to Texas.

He said, "Oh, you want to get rid of me?" then chuckled.

She said, "No, silly, I just want to know how you're coming." Chris said he'd see the doctor in a week and, "I'll see about leaving then." He said he loved being here and getting to see her, but he really wanted to be back in the Navy too. Ashley understood. Chris said he would begin his "pilot" training when he got back, and he was excited about that.

Ashley thought that would be neat to have a fiancé to be training as a pilot. She asked when they could get together again, and Chris told her the doctor said he couldn't drive a car for at least another week because of his severe concussion. She said, "I have a car. I can come and see you." He thought that would be nice.

He said, "Just give me a call and let me know when you're coming." She promised she would. Ashley's mom said she was going shopping for their trip and wanted to know if she wanted to go along.

She said, "Sure, Mom. Just give me a second to change into something a little better." Her mom was surprised, but glad she was going shopping with her. Maybe she'd mention about the night she and Jim went out, as her mom and dad both, really didn't approve of that, but mentioned to each other, "She's old enough to know what she's doing."

Sunday came and Ashley welcomed it. She needed some distraction. Maybe something the pastor would say would help her one way or another. Sunday morning came and Ashley was dressed for church. To her surprise her mom and dad both had their Sunday clothes on. Ashley said, "Is it really true? Are you really going to church with me this morning?"

They both answered, "Yes, we're going. We like what it's doing for you. Maybe it will do something for us." Ashley thought to herself, *If they only knew!* Ashley was pleased to introduce her dad and mom to the pastor. He seemed very happy to meet them, and told them he would be glad to see them again, then the Coopers told him of their extended trip they would be going on, so it would be some time. The pastor wished them a joyous and restful trip and gave them good-byes. Ashley told Pastor Smucker, "You'll be seeing me next Sunday." He told her he was pleased.

They went to a fine restaurant for dinner, then went home and Mom started doing some packing, as they already had their "flight tickets." Ashley went to her bedroom and was glad to be alone with her thoughts. She "deep down" wished Chris were going back to Texas soon, so she wouldn't need to see him until she did much thinking and added "praying, too." That would always help, Pastor

Smucker told her already. She wondered why being in love was so complicated, but then she faced the reality *being in love with just one man wouldn't be complicated.*

As she lay on her bed thinking, she thought if she and Jack were engaged, they would probably be married soon, and for a minute she wished that were true. Then she looked at her engagement ring. She did some sensible thinking. *Maybe if I would tell Chris I was too hasty in becoming engaged and I wanted to give him the ring back that would solve all problems.* At least she could have peace in dating until she really got things sorted out. *Yes, maybe that's what I'll tell Chris when I go see him again.* She knew that would break his heart and especially laying that on him after his accident. Oh, she wished it were simple, but maybe it would be if she only had "faith" to believe it.

A week had passed and Ashley thought it was time she was hearing from Chris, or should she call him? The telephone rang and that startled her thoughts. It was Chris. They talked a while, then Chris told Ashley he would be leaving for the Navy in two days. His doctor said he was in good shape and he could leave. The patch was taken off his forehead, and he was healing nice, and if it would continue so, he might not even need plastic surgery. Chris asked Ashley if he could come see her tomorrow, as the doctor said he could drive now. She said yes, that would be fine, what time? He said around two o'clock. She said that would be great. Then they both "hung up" after saying good-bye and his adding that he missed her. Ashley thought, *I can't tell him now about breaking off the engagement.* It just wasn't the right time until he got back in the "swing of things in the Navy." Then she'd tell him in a letter. She just didn't have the heart to tell him now.

Tomorrow came, and she saw Chris driving up the lane. She went out to meet him. He looked good, and the wound on his forehead looked exceptionally good. He looked so handsome in his Navy uniform, including his hat. She welcomed him in the house after a big hug and kiss. It wasn't hard pretending to love such a tall, handsome guy. One couldn't ask for more. Again, Ashley was getting confused and wondered if she should just wait for him to get a promotion and earn a bigger salary.

The weighty thoughts were interrupted when Chris said, "Ashley, you seem to be in deep thought." She said she was just thinking what a great guy he was, and how handsome. He said he was grateful he had such a beautiful girl who would one day be his forever! He wasn't making it any easier for her. Then she changed the subject by telling him her dad and mom got off on their trip two days ago, and she drove them to Wichita for their flight. He commented on how wonderful it was they could go on such a fine trip. Ashley asked about his travel plans and said she would be glad to take him wherever he left from.

He said, "Thanks, but my mom and dad bought me a plane ticket, instead of one for the bus, and they want to take me to Wichita to board it." Ashley was relieved. That way she wouldn't have to struggle to communicate going down to Wichita. When it was time to leave, Chris gave Ashley a big squeeze and kissed her hard. She returned the favor. It wasn't hard to pretend, either.

Now they were separated for who knows how long. Ashley was glad for the moment, she decided not to break up the engagement, and there was no question in her mind that she loved him a lot. Maybe it would work out.

The mail had come and there was a letter from Samantha. It read, "We hope you're not too lonesome, but Mary and I won't be coming home this weekend, hope you don't mind." Ashley thought, *Oh great, because I want to be alone for a while.* She thought about Jim at K.U. and even thought about Jack in Ohio. She was wishing she would hear from either one of them, but tomorrow was Sunday, and she was eagerly awaiting going to church. She had a blouse she wanted to press before going, so she better get to it. She always dressed real sharp, and her looks alone did everything for her, let alone her attire. Then she thought, *That's being proud, and it says in the Bible, "Pride goeth before destruction."* She remembered her pastor quoting that verse on Sunday when he was preaching on pride. Then she thought, *But God, I am real happy I'm not ugly.* She laughed a little bit at herself.

She was startled when the phone rang, and said, "Now who can that be?" Sure enough, it was Jim calling from K.U. Ashley was delighted to hear his voice and she said, "I just told Chris good-bye a while ago. He is leaving for the Navy and I don't know when I'll be seeing him again."

Jim said, "was it hard telling him good-bye?"

She hesitated, then said, "Yes, it was difficult, it could be a long time before I'll see him again."

Jim was glad in a way, then said, "Would it be possible for me to drive up tomorrow, Sunday, and see you, for old times sake?"

She told him she was going to church in the morning, "But you could come in the afternoon."

He was pleased and said, "Great, I'll be there sometime around 2:00 if that's okay with you?" Ashley informed him she would like that, as she was the only one at home. Her mom and dad had left on their trip. Jim was even more glad for that, he thought. Then Ashley hung up and hurriedly pressed her blouse for church tomorrow and she thought, *That's what I'll wear tomorrow with my new red and black plaid suit, and I'll wear my red boots and take my red purse, too.*

She liked to "dress up" and with a figure like hers, she

could do it, too. She finished pressing her blouse and then she decided to wash her hair. All she needed to do after the shampoo was to dry it, as it was naturally wavy. She was thankful for that.

Sunday came, Ashley awoke early thinking about Jim. She ate a danish and had coffee for breakfast. She didn't need to watch her weight, but she ate sensibly. She dressed and went to church. There were "greeters" at the door and she was welcomed. There were girls there, and boys as well, whom she judged pretty close to her age. Probably some younger and a few older. The girls were attractive and several boys who were quite handsome looking. She never went to Sunday school, just for preaching.

She sat beside a very pretty girl. She became acquainted with her. She was Patricia, Pat for short, and she was the pastor's daughter. They visited a while and then the service began. Ashley didn't have her mind on the sermon very much, as she was thinking about Jim, until Pastor Smucker announced there would be a social in the social room in the church this afternoon between two and four o'clock for the young people only. Refreshments would be provided. This made Ashley "sit up" and "take notice." That was just great, she thought. She and Jim would come and that would break the monotony of them having to visit too much. Oh! She was excited! Before this, she was wondering just what they could do all afternoon, but this solved everything. She told Pat she would be there with a friend of hers and Pat was delighted. She was too excited to eat after she got home from church, but she thought, *oh well they'll have refreshments anyway.* The time seemed to go fast and before she realized it, Jim would soon be there.

When she saw he had arrived, she grabbed her purse and locked the doors and went out to greet him. He said,

"Well, Ashley, you seem happy, what's this all about?" and she told him about the social at church. "It already has started and lasts until four o'clock, isn't that exciting?" Jim "faintly" said, "Yes, it is," but thought he would rather be alone with her, then he said, "Jump in, we're off!" This she did happily. They got there soon and the social had just barely begun. Ashley was ecstatic.

Pat Smucker came up to them and said, "Ashley, is this your friend?"

Ashley delightedly said, "Yes, it is. He is Jim Bennington. He is a medical student at K.U. at Lawrence, Kansas." Pat gripped his hand as if elated he was there. Everyone it seemed was all talking at once until one of the young men brought the meeting to order and welcomed everyone who was there, and especially new faces. He told the new ones there to make themselves known, telling where they were from and what they did. This each one did. There were a handful of new faces. They all played games, which took concentrating, as well as other interesting games, then refreshments were being served in the dining room of the social hall. It was 4:30 when Ashley and Jim said their good-byes and then left. When they got in the car, Jim said, "That was 'fun,' Ashley, but now I have you all to myself." He told her, now he knew why she enjoyed church so much because there were some nice looking young men there.

Then she said, "But don't forget the pretty girls, too." Then each chuckled.

Jim said, "Where to now, Ashley?"

She said, "Why not just drive around for a while, or maybe you have to get back to K.U." He announced he had an hour yet before returning, as he did want to do a little studying yet this evening. Then all of a sudden Jim said, "On the other hand, let's just get you home and talk a while." She consented. There was silence for a few minutes, then Jim said, "Now Ashley, what will be taking up your time since Chris has gone?" Ashley said she had some housework she wanted to do and then her sisters Mary and Samantha would be coming home from college next weekend perhaps. She knew all too well she would be lonely and would like to see Chris and Jack Riley who was in Ohio working in a bank where he was promoted to a higher position. Then Jim looked at his watch and said he better be headed back to K.U. and that he enjoyed the social but he would have liked to have had her all to himself. Ashley was quiet. She got up enough nerve to ask him if he would be coming to see her regularly.

He said, "Only until you ask me to stop."

Ashley said, "I guess that's a fair answer." Then they hugged and gave each other a little kiss and he was gone.

Ashley went upstairs to her room and undressed and got into something comfortable. She then sat down at her desk and started writing Chris a letter. She jumped when she heard the phone ring. It was her mom and dad calling to see how she was getting along. She told them about the afternoon and the good time they had at the church social for young people. Mom and Dad were each on a separate phone and in unison said, "What's that?" She then had to tell them about Jim being there. Before they hung up, her dad said, "Ashley, we have a lot of confidence in you. Be sure your conscience tells you the right thing to do." She assured them it would and for them to not worry, but trust her. After having been assured, they said good-bye and "we love you."

Ashley went back to her letter writing to Chris. Being with Jim this afternoon sort of put a "damper" on knowing just what to write. She knew she loved Chris, but she loved Jim and Jack, too. Now she had to decide which one she loved the most. She knew if she settled for Jack only, they would probably get married in the near future, only she didn't feel like settling down quite yet. She finished Chris's letter, more like a note, as she didn't write much. All of a sudden, she felt fortunate to having three young men who were in love with her. Now she had to choose which one she wanted to settle down with for life. Ashley reread the note she wrote to Chris, then she tore it up. It didn't sound like she was engaged to him, or was wearing his ring. She wasn't in the frame of mind to write Chris, so put off writing until the next day at least. She knew he would become suspicious if she didn't soon write. She promised herself it would be tomorrow, if not before. Maybe that day the mail would have something in it that might get her in the mood.

The mail was late. Ashley kept watching for the mail carrier, finally she saw him coming up the road. She went outside and waited. Sure enough, there was a letter from Chris. She opened the letter hurriedly; halfway through he said, "I became a Lieutenant yesterday. I wanted to call you, but decided to write instead." He said he was very busy, and the next day would be his first "solo flight." Ashley kept reading hurriedly. He went on to tell her he loved her so much and wished she were closer to his training. Then he signed off saying, "Please wait for me, I couldn't bear it if you didn't, love, Chris."

Ashley thought, *I'm so glad I didn't mail the "note" I had written to Chris.* She thought and said aloud, "a Lieutenant." *That's wonderful. He must really be doing good!* Then she was in the mood for letter writing, but first, she reread the letter. It thrilled her to say the least!

The first thing she wrote was, "Congratulations. I'm so proud of you and proud to be wearing your ring," and so she wrote what became two pages long. She got in her car and drove to the post office where she mailed the letter.

She wanted him to get it as soon as possible, and did not want to have to wait until tomorrow to mail it. She was so thrilled over the news, she went shopping for some new clothes, then she went to a restaurant where she had dinner. She didn't want to go home just yet, so she drove around, and as the hour was getting late, she drove home. She felt like calling Mary and Samantha at college and telling them the news. She knew they would be excited, and happy for her, so call she did, and she talked to each of them. They said they were so busy they didn't know when they could get home, but they didn't like leaving her alone so much. They said they promised Mom and Dad they would visit occasionally.

Ashley said it was rather lonely, but Chris and Jim had taken up some of her time. Then they said good-bye and for Ashley to call them if she needed them. Ashley promised to do so.

Ashley woke up to a beautiful sunshiny morning. She wondered what she could do that day, besides tidying up the house. She was eating a bowl of cereal when an idea popped into her mind. She thought, *why don't I call up Pat Smucker, and ask to take her out to lunch?* The more she thought about it, the better she liked the idea and promised herself she would call her after breakfast was over and she finished tidying up the kitchen. So she did.

Pat answered the phone and Ashley said, "Pat, are you busy this noon?"

And Pat thought a minute, then said, "No, nothing pressing." Then Ashley asked if she could come to her house and pick her up and take her out to lunch around eleven o'clock. Pat said, "That sounds very interesting and nice, sure I'd like that." Then they both said good-bye and hung up. Ashley straightened up the kitchen, and odds and ends around the house, then went upstairs to dress. Anything she put on she looked good in. So she grabbed a short skirt, blouse and sweater vest, in case it was cold in the restaurant, as it was prone to be in some she had been in. She planned to take her to a nice place and quiet too, so they could visit.

Ashley was there at 10:45 and Pat was ready to go, and said, "This is nice. I think I'll enjoy this." Then they started to go. Pat looked at Ashley's hand and said, "So you're engaged to the friend you had at the social last Sunday afternoon." This took Ashley "aback."

Then she said, "No, Pat. I'm engaged to a man in the Navy who is a Lieutenant. Jim and I are very good friends. He is at K.U. studying medicine."

Pat was silent for a moment, then said, "Who is the Navy man and how fortunate can you be?"

Ashley told her, "his name is Chris Engle. He lives here in Kansas. He's tall and has black curly hair and is very handsome."

Then Pat said, "I wish I were as fortunate."

Ashley drove up to a nice looking restaurant, and said, "This is it, let's go in." They got inside and Ashley told the hostess, "Could we have a nice quiet place so we can talk?" The hostess took them to just such a place. Ashley thanked her and she and Pat sat down. They were brought a menu; they ordered, then they sat back and started to talk. Ashley took Pat into her confidence, saying, "I'm in love with both men. In fact, I was corresponding with another young man in Ohio whom I was also in love with but wrote him and broke up our corresponding, but still am in love with."

Pat's mouth dropped open, and Ashley told Pat that this was bothering her so much, she knew she could only marry one and she was trying to decide whom she loved the most. Pat asked who the third one was, and Ashley told her, "His name is Jack Riley. He works in a bank in Ohio and not too long ago, he got a big promotion, and he told me, with his promotion, he thinks he will be in shape to marry me. He said this after I broke up corresponding with him, as he loves me a lot." Then Ashley said, "So you see now why I have the problem I do, because I love him too!"

Pat again was silent for a minute, then said, "I should be so fortunate." Then Ashley said she had a lot of faith in her father's preaching and once he counseled her. She said, "He agrees I can and should be with the one I'm engaged to, and he is in training as a Lieutenant Navy pilot." She said, "With Chris, I can't see anything for us in the near future, as his earnings in the Navy aren't too great." Ashley then went on to tell Pat about his accident, flying home with him and so forth. Then Ashley said, "Pat, it's so complicated being in love with three men at the same time." Then she looked directly at Pat, and said, "I'm telling you all this in confidence."

Pat said, "I know. You can rest assured it won't go any further."

Ashley thanked her. Then their meals came and the subject was changed to what Pat was doing and about her love life. Pat said, "I'm dating some young men from our church that you saw at the social, but nothing steady, nor serious." In Ashley's heart she almost wished it was that simple for her. They must have been at the restaurant for at least two hours and both thought they should be going. So they left and Ashley drove Pat home, and when they got there, Ashley said, "Pat, will you pray for me?" Pat promised she would. After Ashley dropped Pat off at her home, she felt a sense of relief that she opened up to Pat about her love life. She had the assurance from Pat that she would keep everything confidential that she told her; for this, she breathed a sigh of relief. She went upstairs to her room as soon as she got inside her home. It seemed as if that were the only quiet place she could truly concentrate. Even though there was no one at home besides her, she still enjoyed her room. This is where she wrote her letters to Chris.

Ashley thought about Jim who was at K.U. studying medicine. She felt sorry for him not having his folks in Kansas any more, as they had moved to Florida a long time back. She thought she was the only one who could get him away from school for a while, and to her home. Her thoughts were interrupted when she heard the phone ring.

She picked up the extension in her room. It was Jim, wanting to know how she was, and how she was getting along being by herself. She told him she was doing fine, but she did feel rather alone. Then she mentioned to him about having taken the pastor's daughter, Pat, out that afternoon for lunch and a nice visit.

Jim said, "Oh, I remember her from the social. She's a nice looking girl." Then it hit Ashley. Maybe he would try and date her and she didn't like that idea very much, but she knew he was free to choose to do as he liked. Then Jim said, "Ashley, are you still there?" And she informed him she was thinking. Jim asked, "Would you care for company Saturday and Sunday?" Right away Ashley thought he would have to stay at her place, and she didn't much like that, and that she wasn't a good cook.

Then she said, "Yes, Jim, I would enjoy your company, but I'm not a good cook, if you can live with that." Jim said, "If you would rather not have me, I could come for Saturday and then leave for school that evening."

Ashley at once said, "Oh no, I don't want you to do that. Please come and stay over Sunday, and we'll go to church together." He thanked her and hung up. Jim was thinking after he "hung up," *I might even get to like one of the girls* who attends church there. Then he thought, *But I don't think I could love any girl like I love Ashley*

At the same time Ashley was thinking, *Jim won't take no for an answer.* But she never said no to him, so why should he? She was glad the spare room was "made up" with clean sheets the last time he was there, but she must do the bathroom and the bedroom and the living room needed a good dusting too. So the next morning she was up early and got to cleaning as he would be there tomorrow, Saturday. She didn't even take time to eat breakfast.

*There, that's done,* she thought, as she finished putting her cleaning essentials away. Then she went out for lunch, and on the way home stopped at a market and bought some groceries for the weekend. She thought they would probably go out and eat one or so meals. She was glad her dad had left her money before they left on their trip, and she also had a small bank account that her dad "opened up" for her before they left on their trip. She thought she really was fortunate to have a dad and mom like hers. She was aware she didn't take advantage of it though. Then Ashley was thinking, *Jim could just as well date one of the girls at church. They were all nice looking.* She thought, *How would I feel if Jim dated one of the girls?* She wouldn't much like it. She felt terrible then, she had three young men who loved her and she wanted to keep them all. She didn't like herself very much. Then she thought, *I can't have them all, sooner or later, I'm going to have to choose one, and only one, but which one?* Then she looked at her engagement ring. She really had decided on Chris, as she was wearing his ring. She knew in her heart if Chris could marry her soon she would surely marry him, but really, how long would it be?

Then she thought of Jack in Ohio who would marry her before long if she were engaged to him. "Oh, why did I break up corresponding with him?" she said aloud. She shook herself a bit and thought, *I've got to get ready for Jim. He's coming soon.* And just how would it be, just the two of them in the house alone? She knew it would be awkward.

Then she prayed, "Dear God, help me this weekend to make a decision."

Saturday was really here, and she hurriedly made a tuna casserole; that was easy, and she had vegetables for a salad, but what for dessert? Then she thought, *We could go out for refreshments. Oh well, I'll just play it by ear.*

Jim arrived and she went to the door to welcome him. He looked as handsome as ever, holding his overnight bag. She took him to his room, but he already had slept there, so he knew where it was. Anyway, she took him to it, and told him she hoped he would sleep comfortably. He assured her he would.

Ashley then went downstairs to put the casserole in the oven for approximately fifteen minutes, and was making a salad when Jim came down from upstairs.

He went into the kitchen and saw Ashley busy at work and said, "Here, let me help you. I'm good at making salads." So she let him take over while she set the table. All the time she was somewhat nervous. Everything was ready and they sat down at the table.

Ashley said, "Do you want to pray Jim and give thanks for the food, or should I?"

Jim said, "You do it, Ashley." Then she took his hand and held it while she said a little prayer for the meal.

Ashley apologized for not having dessert and mentioned maybe they could go for a drive and have refreshments out. Jim assured her that would be fine. The dishes were put in the dishwasher and they went to the living room and talked.

Jim said, "Ashley, you handled that well. I thought you

were a little nervous. If my folks had not moved to Florida, we wouldn't be in this position."

Ashley said, "Yes. I was a bit shaken up, but you did your best to put me at ease, and that helped." They talked a while longer, then decided to go for a drive. Jim, as usual, put her in the driver's seat and then got in beside her. She never moved over, so they sat very close to each other.

They chatted and then there was a drugstore, when Ashley said, "We can go in there for dessert if you like."

Jim said, "If you don't mind, I'd just as soon drive. Your lunch was satisfying, and I had plenty." She thanked him and they drove in silence for a while before either talked. Then they realized it was time to go home. Jim helped her out on his side, and then he planted a little kiss on her cheek. She was expecting that and wished that the night was over. It was Sunday morning. Jim came downstairs in his good suit and tie, he looked so handsome. Ashley wasn't ready for church yet, as she fixed breakfast. It didn't take long to clean up the dishes, and then she excused herself and went upstairs to get dressed for church. She came down and when Jim saw her, he whistled. She was embarrassed. They had one and one-half hours before leaving for church, so they went into the living room and talked.

Jim said, "Ashley, I wish you were wearing my engagement ring."

Ashley said, "Jim, we have to talk." Jim listened. "You know I shouldn't even be seeing you. I'm engaged to Chris Engle. By the way, he was promoted to a Lieutenant."

Jim said, "Oh, he must be doing something right."

Ashley smiled a wee smile and then added, "We should not even be together now."

Jim said, "If you didn't want me here, you could have said, don't come." Ashley knew he was right.

Then Ashley said, "Jim, I'm in love with you, too."

He said, "I thought as much. What are you going to do about it?"

Ashley said, "It will be some time before I see Chris, and I'm lonely with Mom and Dad gone, and Mary and Samantha both in college, and they don't get home very often." Then she added, "You know I broke up corresponding with Jack in Ohio, and he still loves me and would soon marry me if I agreed."

Jim listened. "Is that what you want Ashley, to get married? If it is, I would marry you in a minute."

She said, "No. I don't want to get married just yet, but it will be a long time before Chris and I can get married. He as much as said so, and I'm not sure I can wait that long." Then she was surprised when she found herself saying, "I could break up my engagement to him. I love him, but I love you and Jack too."

Jim was silent, then said, "Would you do that for me, and not be sorry when it was over?"

Ashley said, "I have to make up my mind, but I don't want to be sorry. I'm afraid if I do break up with Chris, he'll think it's because he is in no position to get married for some time, and that would break his heart." Then she added, "Jim, let's don't see each other for a while, not even correspond and maybe I can decide what I really want."

Jim said, "Maybe that's the way we should handle it." They talked so long and were reminded by the clock that church had already started and they would walk in late. Ashley hated to do that, as it would be "obvious," but they decided to go anyway.

After church was over, Pat came up to them and said, "It is nice to see you two again."

They both smiled, then Ashley said, "Pat, you remember Jim?" Pat nodded her head. Ashley saw Jim give her the "once over." In a way Ashley was glad. The two of them visited a lot and then the other young people, men as well as girls, came up and spoke to them both, and reacquainted themselves. Then Ashley did it! She told them the ring was from another man, that Jim was a very good friend. Then the girls really took notice, and it became obvious.

They said they should be going, and Jim said, "Maybe we'll see each other again." Ashley in her mind knew it was over for Jim and her. In a way she was relieved. They got in Jim's car and headed out for a restaurant.

Jim said, "This is on me." Ashley smiled. Dinner was over and they headed for home. Jim went upstairs and changed into something more comfortable, and he said, "Well, I guess I better go. And, Ashley, if this is the end for us, know in your heart, I still love you."

Ashley said, "it's mutual." They embraced for a long time and kissed and Jim was off. Ashley watched until his car was out of sight. She didn't even cry. She went upstairs, sat down at her desk, and wrote her fiancé a letter. Ashley felt good in her heart that she did the right thing. Her heart was really in the letter she was writing Chris. Again she signed her letter, "your future wife" and "all my love, Ashley."

# Chapter 4

The next morning was a lonely day, she felt. She got in her car and drove to the post office to drop Chris's letter off, as she was anxious to get it to him. There was warmth in the letter that had never been there before. She hoped Chris would feel it too. She thought, *Now what am I going to do to fill up my time?* Then she thought of Janet, her sister who was working as a maid in rich people's homes in California. She was tempted to go out West and try it, and if she didn't like it, she could come back home. She also thought she could stop in Texas on the way out to see Chris, but would she have to call him first and see if and when, she could see him. She would leave her car at home and fly out, as she didn't want that long trip alone. Then she would have to call Mary and Samantha at K. State and let them know, as the house would be unoccupied, with her mom and dad on their extended trip. She was going around in circles, knowing everything she would have to do, and then getting her air flight and all. She didn't know how she would get to Wichita to board the plane. She would have to think of something. She already did. Jim would be delighted to drive her to Wichita, but would that be right after having broken up their corresponding. She called Jim anyway, and he was in class, so she left a message for him to call her as soon as he could. Now she would call the airport and get a ticket. So many things were hounding her about the whole trip.

First she would have to get in touch with Chris before she bought her ticket, and that would be complicated, his being in the Navy. She never knew what time to call him. She didn't know what time he would be in, possibly this evening would catch him in, so she decided to wait, and then when she got him, perhaps the plane ticket would be hard to schedule. Maybe it would be best not to stop over in Texas. *Oh, there are so many things to do and what would be the best to do first?* She was getting confused and she knew that wouldn't help the situation, being in that frame of mind. She knew she could call her sisters at K. State and get that over with. So she went to get their phone number and placed a call. How fortunate, Mary was in her room with her next class in a couple of hours. This gave Ashley time to lay everything on the line and tell her all the plans that were troubling her and ask which to do first. Mary asked if she wanted her to come home and help her through all this. Ashley was tempted, but said, "No, not just yet. I need to get in touch with Chris first of all."

They talked a while, and then Mary said, "If you get in a tight fix, don't be afraid to call." Either she or Samantha would perhaps be available. Ashley told her thanks, and she just may do that, and hung up. Chris had given Ashley a number to call in case of an emergency.

She thought, *This is an emergency, so I'll call this evening.* Ashley called the number Chris gave her to call and the one who answered the phone said he was out in training but he would be glad to take a message. So Ashley gave her number to have Chris call her that evening or when it was convenient, and thanked whoever was on the phone. She felt good she got that much accomplished. Now she just would wait. The phone rang at last. It was Chris on the line.

Right away he asked if something was wrong. Then she

told him of her plans. He was surprised she was planning to go to California to work, and asked if he had anything to do with that. At once she assured him he didn't. She was getting bored and wanted to do something gratifying for a change. Chris understood and said he thought that would be "fine, if that's really what you want." She said she would be able to see her sister Janet occasionally, too. Then Chris told her he was in helicopter training and had so many hours to put in before he could fly solo. He thanked her for thinking of him, but his time was especially full and he couldn't tell her when he could get away, especially since it would be hard getting around without a car. He said he was sorry, but it might not be such a good idea to stop on the way out. He said he was having a break just before he was flying solo and right now he couldn't tell her when.

Ashley was upset and Chris could tell by her voice she was upset. He said, "Ashley darling, I love you so much, and if there was a possibility of getting away, I sure would."

Ashley said, "Maybe that's for the best," so she'd go right through without stopping, except when she changed planes in Chicago. Then she added she would write him when she got settled in California, and asked him if he had received her letter.

He said, "No, when did you write?" She told him a few days ago and that he might get it today. Then they said good-bye and hung up.

Ashley was upset with Chris that he couldn't make time for her, but maybe that's the way being in training was. Ashley thought and said aloud, "He may be sorry when he reads my letter," and hoped he was. She then called the airport and asked for reservations to California. She got them as she suspected with a three-hour wait in Chicago. She wasn't happy about that. Ashley thought, *Now I must call Jim about a ride to Wichita airport.* He was in class when she called, but she left a message for him to call her. Then she went upstairs and got clothes around that she wanted to pack. She got her best suit laid out to wear when Jim picked her up, as she wanted to make an impression. She realized she was still very much in love with him. She packed her lightweight suitcase and cosmetic case, besides her "carry-on" bag. By now she was getting excited about her trip, and she felt upset with Chris for not having made time for her in passing through. This made her want to see Jim more than ever, and she knew it wasn't over yet. The phone rang. It was Jim. "Hello, beautiful," he said.

"It's a nice surprise you calling me, and what can I do for you?" Ashley broke down and cried. She apologized for crying, but said she'd been under such pressure it had to come out. Then she told him everything. Even about Chris not getting off to see her when she went through Texas, but now she was flying straight through with the exception of a stop in Chicago to change planes. She then told him she had a big favor to ask him, and "Please say if you can't make it."

After she asked him, Jim said, without hesitation, "Tell me when you want me to be there and I'll be there." So she told him what time the plane leaves and Jim was figuring how long the trip would take from her place to Wichita, and they decided on a time. Rather, Jim did, and said, "Don't worry about getting there late. I figure plenty of time to check in your luggage and everything else. I'll see you, Ashley, and thanks again for calling me," and they hung up.

Ashley broke down and had a long cry. She was so "up tight" about everything, and now it was really happening, so she just "let go" for a while and couldn't help it. She felt better after her cry. She dried her tears and went to the kitchen to fix herself a sandwich. She realized she barely ate a thing all day, and she better start taking care of herself. She knew Jim would tell her that too, being a doctor. She was so grateful for Jim. Then she said, "Dear God, thanks for working things out so well."

She went to look for her house keys to lock everything up. She knew her folks and sisters at K. State had a set too. So that was off her mind, then she went to bed very relaxed, but tired.

Several days had gone by. *Tomorrow I leave for California,* she thought. Morning came and Ashley was up early. She hurriedly got dressed, skipped breakfast, as she had last minute things to do. She looked at her watch. Jim would be there any minute. She put her luggage, cosmetic case, and bag by the door so as not to forget anything. She saw Jim driving up.

She met him at the door, and the first thing he said was, "Ashley, what gives?" She said she would explain to him on the way. They better get started now, to have plenty of time at the airport before the plane leaves. They were settled and on their way. Jim said, "I'm waiting, Ashley."

Ashley started at the beginning and when she finished, she said, "You see why I'm a little keyed up?"

Jim said, "Chris may be busy, but how could he not have the time for his fiancée?" Then he said, "I would think even the Navy could get off that long."

Ashley said, "I'm wondering if I picked the wrong guy." She was really indebted to Jim for doing this for her. Then she said, "Jim, I want to continue to correspond with you when I'm in California, if it's not too late." Jim assured her he would be more than happy to correspond with her. Ashley was honest with Jim and said, "I'm not even sure now where I stand with Chris, maybe he is that busy, I don't want to misjudge him." Well, anyway, the matter was dropped and they talked about the lighter things, such as being thrilled she would be doing something in California both girls worked. She asked the stewardess when the plane was to land in L.A. The stewardess said in about thirty minutes. She was glad everything went so well at the Chicago airport. Thirty minutes didn't give Ashley very much time to think what she would do, but first thing she had to do was get her suitcase. Hopefully it would be there when she got there. She heard of people not having their suitcases when the plane arrived.

She breathed a prayer, "Dear God, let my suitcase be there when I arrive." The plane arrived and she was up close to the entrance, she was glad of that. She finally was off and what a crowd of people there to welcome the people who had arrived. Now she was wishing she had called Janet to meet her there. She got her suitcase, which she was thankful was there, and she said, "God, thank you."

Then she asked someone at the desk where she could find a telephone. There was one close by for which she was thankful. She set her luggage down and got Janet's telephone number. She called and the line was busy. She waited several minutes, and called again. She was thankful when she heard the phone ring. How fortunate could she be? Janet answered, and Ashley told her where she was, which about floored Janet, and Ashley wondered if she could possibly come and get her. Janet said, "Just a minute." Janet told the lady whom she works for what it was all about.

It happened the man of the house was also there, and he said to Janet, "Come on, I'll drive you there. This is a busy time of day. You better not drive in all that traffic." She asked the lady of the house if it was all right for her to take off for an hour or so. She was lonely. Janet had written to her mom and dad how nice they were to her, and how much they liked her. So she wasn't surprised.

Ashley told Janet where she would be, in front of the

that she thought she'd enjoy, "anyway, if it doesn't work out, I can always quit."

"Here we are," said Jim, at the airport. She was flying United, so Jim dropped her off there and left her there with her luggage while he went and parked.

Ashley said, "Jim, you don't need to wait for the plane if you're in a hurry to get back to K.U."

Jim said, "I took the day off. I'll make it up when I get back." Ashley was pleased. Everything was in order, ticket checked, luggage checked in, and she still had time for a cup of coffee. Jim told Ashley to send her address when she got located. She promised he would be the first to know. That pleased Jim.

Jim looked at his watch and said, "Ashley, we better get over there where you board the plane. It's almost time." Ashley agreed. Then they announced over the loudspeaker for the people to start loading. Jim and Ashley gave each other big squeeze and a lengthy kiss.

She was out of sight and hollered back, "Thanks a million, Jim, for everything." Jim heard her faintly. He stayed and watched the plane take off and until it was out of sight. Then he slowly walked to where his car was parked. He had a long and lonely trip back to K.U.

Ashley was busy with her thoughts. She had the assurance Jim was the one for her now and not Chris. Then she settled back to relax when lunch was served. She was hungry, as she didn't eat breakfast. She had a nice lunch, very satisfying. Then she closed her eyes and relived again the time with Jim. She thought, *It took that to set me on the right track.* Ashley was thinking she should have called her sisters before she left home. Then when she got into Los Angeles, she had her sister's number with her. She also had her friend's number. She had her sister Janet's address. She could just take a taxi to Pasadena, as that was where

United Airways. Ashley thanked her and was thrilled something good had happened to her, so maybe she had made the right decision to go out to L.A. to work. Ashley then thought, *I can't stay there. Where will I stay?* Maybe Janet had an answer for that, hopefully.

Then Ashley went to get some coffee and went to a quiet place to wait for her sister. People started coming toward where she was sitting to board an outgoing plane, but at least she was sitting down, and had a long wait ahead of her. She made good connections on the whole flight. God was certainly good to her, she thought. Then her mind went to Jim. She would write him just as soon as she was located. She never even thought about Chris, until she looked down at her ring. An hour had gone by and Janet still wasn't there, so she waited. She thought of her Pastor Monroe and how he mentioned having faith in God. So she just breathed a sigh and was thankful Janet was there when she called. It could have been her day off or something else, so she was aware of how good God was to her and she prayed a quiet little prayer for God's goodness to her.

All of a sudden someone said, "Ashley." It was Janet. The girls embraced each other, and Janet introduced her boss, Mr. Sterling, to her. He made her feel welcome at once. He picked up Ashley's suitcase and cosmetic case and led them to the car, while Janet and she talked and talked. They were at the car, a Lincoln Continental. But Ashley wasn't surprised, the way Janet's letters read.

They were home at last, and Mr. Sterling said, "Ashley, you are going to stay here until you find a place to work."

Ashley said, astounded, "Oh no, I couldn't do that. I don't want to be a burden."

He said, "Yes, Mrs. Sterling is already getting a room prepared for you to stay."

Ashley with tears in her eyes said, "What can I say? You're so lovely and accommodating."

He said, "We think the world of Janet, and we sure want to be of help to her sister."

They were in the house, and then Mrs. Sterling gave her a lovely greeting, and said, "This is your house as long as you need it."

Ashley threw her arms around her, and with tears in her eyes, she said, "You are too kind, but thank you." Ashley later found out from Janet they were regular church attenders. Neither smoked nor used foul language.

Then Ashley said, "You are so fortunate, Janet. I hope I am so fortunate."

Then Janet said to Ashley, "The Sterling's have friends who are looking for a maid," and they would take her over to meet them tomorrow. Ashley was astounded. Surely God was answering her prayers and she was thankful. Vera Sterling told Janet not to fix dinner, as they would all be eating out tonight to celebrate Ashley's coming. Janet was overjoyed. Then Mrs. Sterling took Ashley to her room. It was exotic, to say the least. Then she told Janet to take the afternoon off and to help Ashley unpack and to just enjoy each other.

The girls had much to talk about. Janet saw Ashley's ring, and said, "Tell me, Ashley, all about your love life." They talked for hours until the Sterlings announced they would be going out for dinner in an hour. The girls thanked them and both got ready. Ashley took a quick shower and put something attractive on. Janet was dressed attractively, too. When the girls were downstairs, Mr. Sterling said, "What beautiful sisters you both are. Your folks sure know how to raise them." The girls gave a quiet little giggle and said, "Thank you."

Ashley and Janet talked for several hours and then

they retired for the night; however, Ashley sat down and wrote Jim a letter, telling him how the trip went and all about getting to Janet's place of work, about the Sterlings' kindness and then how grateful she was to him for all he did for her. She said she loved him even more, if that were possible. She told him she was thinking of sending Chris's ring back and breaking up their relationship. She said what she had once felt for Chris was gone. She went on to tell him she was going to an interview with friends of the Sterlings, as they were looking for a maid, and she hoped they were as nice as the Sterlings, that she would let him know what developed, and in the meantime for him to send his letters to Janet's address. Then she closed with, "Jim, I love you so much, it is something I never felt before, and I know it's real, all my love, Ashley." She then went to bed, exhausted, and must have gone to sleep immediately.

The household was up around seven o'clock the next morning, including Ashley. She watched Janet fix breakfast for the Sterlings, and then they ate in the kitchen, which the maid usually does. After breakfast was over, Mrs. Sterling told Ashley she was going to call her friends and tell them about her, a sister to Janet, and make an appointment for them to interview her. She did this and it suited her friends that afternoon. Mrs. Sterling told Ashley, and said she would like them, as they are so kind and she said if she was a sister to Janet, she's got to be all right. Mrs. Sterling took Ashley to the appointment and all went well, although she told them she couldn't cook like Janet did, due to helping her Dad with the farm work instead of being in the kitchen. The lady said she would help her in the kitchen whenever necessary. They shook hands and left.

Ashley was hired and would start work the following Monday, which gave Ashley several days at the Sterlings to watch Janet work. Ashley told Janet she had to write

Chris and was going to break off their engagement. She hardly knew how to go about it, due to the last letter she wrote Chris. It was a real "love letter." She wished she could talk to her dad, or to Pastor Smucker, but she couldn't, so she prayed, "Dear God, I definitely feel I should break my engagement to Chris and send his ring back. Help me to write the right words. Amen."

She then got out her stationary and began to write. "I am returning your ring because I don't feel towards you as I once did. It was a mistake. I am returning your ring. I hope it gets to you safely." Ashley tore up the letter; she wasn't in the right frame of mind to write now. *Later, I will, though,* and she went downstairs to see if she could help Janet with her chores. Before this, however, she took off the ring and put it in her bag in a coin purse. She would send it back, she promised herself that. Janet had everything under control, her work, that is, so she made Ashley and herself a cup of hot tea. That is just what Ashley needed. It seemed to relax her and she could think better. She showed Janet her hand and Janet said, "The ring is gone."

Ashley said, "Yes, I'm returning it. Do you have a small box I can send it back in?" Janet said she didn't, but she knew Mrs. Sterling could help her out, and she did more than that. She even helped Ashley wrap it. Ashley thanked her and said, "Now it's ready for the post office to be mailed," but first she knew she had to prepare Chris for it coming back.

Meantime Chris in Texas was wondering if Ashley got to California. He felt bad he hadn't made an effort to see her on her way back, but it was hard to schedule a time to get off and see her. He was hoping Ashley would call him when she arrived there. He didn't hear from her and he was becoming anxious. *She may call tonight, he told himself. Ashley did call, but it wasn't the call he expected. She decided to call him instead of writing, so she did. Someone answered and said Chris was there, "Just a minute." He went to the phone relieved that she had called. Ashley told Chris that she arrived in California safely, and that Janet's boss met her at Los Angeles airport and took her to their home where Janet worked and she would begin her new job Monday morning. Chris was happy about that; but she didn't sound like herself.*

Then Ashley said, "Chris, I'm sending the ring back. It was a mistake. I don't feel towards you like I did."

There was a pause, and Chris said, "Don't you love me any more? Was it because I didn't make an effort to see you flying back?"

Ashley said, "Yes, that is part of it, but I don't love you any more." Another pause. Ashley said, "I am deeply in love with Jim. Your ring is packed and you'll be getting it soon."

Chris said, "My God, could your feelings for me change so quickly?"

Ashley said, "They did, that's all I know. I better hang up. I'm using the Sterlings' phone. Nice knowing you and I hope you enjoy your life in the Navy. Good-bye."

Ashley thought, *Was I too abrupt with Chris? Anyway, he knows I don't love him any more.* Now she had to talk to Mrs. Sterling about using her phone for long distance. Mrs. Sterling came out to the kitchen to see how lunch was coming. They had dinner in the evening.

When she started to go in the living room, Ashley said, "Mrs. Sterling, I used your phone to call long distance."

Before she could say any more, Mrs. Sterling said, "Oh, didn't Janet tell you? She has her own private phone and that call will be billed to her phone."

Ashley said, "Oh, I guess Janet forgot to tell me." Mrs. Sterling thanked her anyway. Then Ashley told Janet what Mrs. Sterling said and she just forgot to mention it to her. So Ashley said, "Be sure to mention it to her." So Ashley said, "Be sure and tell me how much my call was so I can pay you."

Janet said she would, then told her, "When you get settled in your new job, be sure and ask the people for your private phone. It's so handy and I can call Mom and Dad and anyone else when I want to." Ashley agreed that was a great idea and she was thinking, *I can call Jim then.* Tomorrow Ashley would get settled in her place of work. She was already getting nervous about it, and wondered just what would be expected of her. She hoped they were as nice as Janet's folks to work for. Janet and Ashley gave each other a big hug. Then Mr. Sterling was waiting to take her to her new job.

He told Ashley, "Don't be nervous. They're really nice people and two of our best friends. We get together often, and we know them well. They, too, are regular church attenders." Ashley was glad to hear that, and thanked Mr. Sterling for all he did for her. Mr. Sterling carried Ashley's suitcase and cosmetic case in the house, and Mrs. Worth was pleased to meet her. Mr. Sterling told Ashley, "I'm sure everything will work out fine," and left. Ashley thanked him.

Then Mrs. Worth told Ashley, "The first thing we're going to do is order you a uniform." Then Ashley remembered Janet wore a uniform. So Ashley gave Mrs. Worth, Arlene, her measurements. Mrs. Worth told Ashley, "You are easy to fit." Then she showed her the run of the house, and all she'd be required to do and that she'd have every Wednesday off and every fourth weekend off.

Ashley said, "Oh, that's wonderful. Janet has the same days off."

Arlene said, "I know. I figured you girls will want the same days off, that is why I made it that way." Ashley thanked her. After Mrs. Worth showed Ashley around the house and told her what would be expected of her, she said, "Now Ashley, we are all, including you, going out to dinner this evening, so you can have the afternoon off to unpack and do what you care to do." Then Ashley asked about having her private phone, as she would be making some long distance calls.

Mrs. Worth said, "I already have that set up for you too, as Mrs. Sterling said Janet enjoys that privilege." Ashley thanked her kindly. Then Ashley unpacked and she saw Jack Riley's phone number and address there, as well as Jim Bennington's. She wondered why she brought Jack's along. She still hadn't gotten over Jack, the one she had met at a church convention in Ohio, although she broke up corresponding with him. Ashley unpacked, laid out her clothes to wear for dinner that evening with the Worths, then she lay down on the bed to relax and do some heavy thinking.

# Chapter 5

Dad and Mom Cooper were home from their trip "around the world." They had a delightful time, but were glad to be home. They called Mary and Samantha at K. State University in Manhattan, Kansas. They were both busy but fine. They asked if Ashley had gotten off to California. This was a surprise to the Coopers, as they hadn't heard she was going. So they called Janet who was working there to see if she heard from Ashley. Janet was surprised to hear they were home from their trip and told them, "Ashley is out here working as a maid and is doing just great." She then went into detail and told them all about her and gave them her telephone number. So Mom and Dad called Ashley and she was also surprised they were home. She told them about her job and that she felt worth something at last. Dad Cooper told her they were putting the farm on the market to sell and are moving to the city of Abilene. They had enough time to think on their trip and felt it was time he retired.

Ashley was excited and glad for them. She told them she broke off her engagement to Chris and sent his ring back, that it was a mistake getting engaged to him in the first place, and that she would write them and tell them all about it. Mom and Dad heard such peace in her voice and were so proud of both her and Janet. Then they hung up.

Dad Cooper said to his wife, Ellen, "We have a lot to be thankful for, our four daughters are doing so well."

Then Ellen said to her husband, Clarence, "I can't quite imagine Ashley working as a maid, doing housework, working on the farm most of her life. She must have a patient and kind lady to work for, but then Ashley will pick it up quickly."

That's just what was happening. Mrs. Worth was very patient to help Ashley in the kitchen, and the cleaning was easy compared to what Ashley did at home off and on. Ashley realized this was good training for her to be someone's wife some day. The mail came and Mrs. Worth took a package out to the kitchen where Ashley was and told her that her uniform came today. They would go upstairs to try it on. The uniform fit perfectly, a white blouse, an orange print skirt, a tiny white apron edged in lace, and a small white cap for her head. Ashley was proud of her outfit and liked all her clothes to fit well, and this one sure did.

Mrs. Worth was happy too and said, "Now I'm going to order two more outfits just like this one." Ashley was pleased. It looked like Janet's, but a different color. Ashley had two hours in the afternoon on her own when lunch was over and the kitchen was immaculate. Ashley kept house like she clothed herself, very neat. Mrs. Worth felt so fortunate to have someone so neat.

During Janet and Ashley's time off in the afternoons, they would call each other up and talk by phone. Janet was very interested in knowing about Ashley's uniform. The girls each had a room at the place where they worked that was theirs to entertain their friends in. Since Janet got a car, the girls planned to get together some afternoon to chat, or go for a drive before they had to return to their places of work to fix dinner for the Sterlings and the Worths. They mainly discussed their mom and dad's retirement and settling in the town of Abilene.

Ashley figured Jim didn't have her letter yet with her

address, so she planned to call him that evening and give it to him. Also she wanted to give him her telephone number. Dinner was over and the kitchen and dining rooms were tidied up, so Ashley went to her room and called Jim. How fortunate could she be? Jim answered the phone and when he heard Ashley's voice, he said, "Hello, beautiful."

Ashley said, "I miss you, but I have a very good job working as a maid for the Worths. They are so nice to work for and I'm really getting the hang of it. I'm learning to cook and I make delicious dishes, which Mrs. Worth is teaching me, and some day I'm going to be a good wife to some young man."

Jim said, "Go on, I'm listening."

Ashley said, "I want that young man to be you, Jim." After Ashley said that, she thought, "What have I done? It is so nice to be free and here I am proposing."

Jim said, "Ashley, I want to marry you. I want to hear you say you're mine. Will you honey?"

Ashley said, "Jim, I shouldn't have said that. I just blurted it out. I just canceled my engagement with Chris. I need to be free for a while, and make sure what I'm doing will be the right thing." Ashley said, "Jim, I love you but I want to give it a little time, and not rush into anything just yet. I need more time. I am your sweetheart, but we should not become engaged just yet. Jim, do you understand?"

Jim was quiet for a few seconds, then said, "Okay, just so we can be sweethearts. That will have to suffice for the time being. Let's continue to correspond and call each one up occasionally. Ashley, will you do that?"

Ashley said, "Of course, I'd like that." Then they talked about medicine and being a maid, and finally told each other good-bye. Ashley admitted to herself she was spoiled. She wanted her cake and eat it too, "naturally speaking." Then she noticed Jack Riley's letter in the dresser door and took it out.

She thought to herself. *I'm not engaged, I could write to Jack, or call him up and tell him where I am and what I'm doing. I'm free, I'm not engaged. It is too late to call him now anyway. I'll see what happens. Maybe I'll give him a call.*

Pastor Monroe Smucker called Clarence and Ellen Cooper to ask about Ashley, as she hadn't been to church for some time and he was concerned about her. They told him all about her and also that she broke her engagement to Chris Engle. He was surprised, but said, under the circumstances he thought she did the right thing and that he'd be praying for her. Then the pastor asked about their trip and they talked a long time about that. They also told him about their putting the farm up for sale. "In fact, it's already on the market," that they're moving to the city of Abilene, as they're retiring. Pastor Smucker wished them well and asked if he could have Ashley's telephone number. He'd like to call her or even have her address to write to her sometime. He told the Coopers they had a lovely daughter and he missed not seeing her pretty face in church. This they did, and then hung up.

Clarence and Ellen started, shortly after they got home from their trip, looking for a home in Abilene. They planned to have a sale for all his machinery, which was much, and all in very good condition. They might even sell some of the furniture. It also was, or is in very good condition. Ellen thought she would miss her house, as it was all modern and she had taken very good care of everything. She wished one or two of the daughters would be home to help out, but she was pleased with all their four daughters and what each were doing.

Mom and Dad Cooper went out a lot to eat, especially dinner. They figured it cost about as much to buy groceries and fix a big meal as it did to go out and eat their dinners. The phone rang and interrupted their talking and thinking. It was Mary from K. State University. She wondered how they were getting along and that they, she and Samantha, had their "spring break" in two weeks and then they would be home to help get ready for the sale. Mom Cooper was happy and said, "That sounds just wonderful," unless they had sold the farm by then; but even then they could help get packed to move into town. So it was let go at that, and Mom thanked her for thinking of them and hung up. The realtors told the Coopers they should have a good sale, as everything was in such good condition.

Pastor Smucker gave Ashley a call the next day after he had her telephone number. Ashley answered and was greatly surprised to hear his voice and she told him so. He was pleased. Then Ashley gave him the details about her job and about the people she worked for, and told him they were just great to work for. Then he asked about her love life, as he thought Ashley wouldn't mind telling him. She told him she broke her engagement to Chris and sent back his ring and it was nice to be free again. She did say however, she had two other fellows whom she loved very much and still can't say how she feels about Chris. Then Pastor Smucker thanked her for being so honest and gave her some sound advice. He told her he thought it was good she broke off with Chris and to not rush into anything just yet. She thanked him for the advice and said good-bye and they both hung up.

After Pastor Smucker hung up, he promised himself he was going to write to Ashley and give her a little more something solid to stand on, and also to remember to pray for her. Ashley was surprised but pleased to hear from her pastor "back home." She decided too, it would be best to not rush into anything just yet anyway. She was tired, as she had a lot on her mind that day, as she served dinner to the Worths' friends that evening. She was thankful too, that they had a dishwasher, as they did in her home. Then she dressed and retired for the night, as morning came too soon to suit her sometimes. She realized she was working on a time schedule, as when she wasn't at home, she pretty much did the way she pleased. She realized this too, was good for her and was glad that she was learning to adjust. Before she knew it, she had drifted off to sleep.

Janet, who worked for the Sterlings, awoke and dressed for work. She and Ashley were going out for a drive in the afternoon on their two-hour break. She was looking forward to that as they hadn't seen each other for nearly two weeks now, although they chatted by phone some. Lunch was over, the dishes cleaned and put away, and the dining room carpet swept and all was done, so Janet went to her room to dress, as she was going to pick up Ashley and go for a drive. Ashley's car was back home in Abilene, Kansas. She wished so much she had it here, then she wouldn't have to depend on Janet and taxicabs to take her around. Janet pulled up in the Worths' driveway and waited on Ashley to come out. "Oh, there she is, she's on time."

They decided to not go anywhere specifically, just drive and talk. They loved the palm trees in California. They talked about boyfriends and Ashley asked Janet if she had one she liked very much.

She said, "No, I'm not as fortunate as you, Ashley." Then they talked about Chris and what made her, Ashley, want to break up with him so suddenly. Ashley told her why, something she never told a single soul, not even Pat Smucker, the pastor's daughter. Janet told her maybe he did have a good excuse for not meeting her. "You know, without a car one can't do much, especially when one is in the 'service' of any kind." Ashley admitted she was too hard with Chris when she talked to him last and was feeling bad about that. She thought she should call him, or write him a letter, but she still didn't have feelings for him like she once did. She said at least she was free now to date and to correspond. She said, however, she really did like Jim and also Jack Riley, whom she had met at a convention in Ohio, and was "toying" with the idea of calling him or writing him a letter and tell him where she is and what she's doing.

They came to a drugstore and Janet said, "I'm hungry for a soda. Shall we go in?" Ashley agreed and said they had an hour yet before they have to get back to the Sterlings and the Worths to fix dinner. So they went in, ordered something, and told them to hurry, as they were on a time schedule. Thus, they were served promptly.

Janet said, "Ashley, you could share one of the three men with me."

And Ashley said, "The problem is, I don't know who I'd let go." She said she knew she was selfish and she thought it really was Jim whom she loved the most. They finished their sodas and started back to their places of work. Ashley got out of the car and thanked Janet for the use of her car and said that she had to do something about not having a car. They said good-bye and Janet "took off." Both Janet and Ashley went upstairs to undress and put on their uniforms to fix dinner.

Mrs. Worth came into the kitchen and told Ashley there was a phone call for her, a young man, and he said he would call back this evening. Ashley thanked her for the message and was thinking about who it was. She couldn't wait until her work was finished for the day and hopefully he would call this evening. She knew she must not neglect her duties of fixing dinner. So she put the call "on hold" and dismissed the call for the time being. She had a simple menu for dinner. When they had something Ashley knew nothing about, Mrs. Worth was always in the kitchen teaching her. Ashley was pleased with the new dishes she was learning to prepare. Indeed she was excited about her job and put everything she had in it.

The Worths were now finished with dinner and Ashley had to "clean up." Then she would go to her room and patiently wait for the call. The phone rang and Ashley jumped with excitement and answered it. It was none other than Jim, whom she more or less expected it was. Her heart was racing when he said, "Hello, beautiful."

Ashley told him she and Janet were out driving this afternoon and was sorry she missed his call. Jim said, "I'm glad you were out with your sister and not a man."

Ashley said, "Silly, who would I be out with here in California?"

He then said, "Don't you get around?"

And Ashley said, "I have a job to do and really that's my priority now."

Jim said, "Yes, but afternoons are free." Ashley told him she knew only Janet and her friend who was out there working, and she hadn't even gotten in touch with her yet, but she wanted to, soon. Then she mentioned about not having her car out there and she had to depend on Janet and taxicabs.

Jim said, "If I wasn't too busy, I'd drive it out to you, but I honestly can't get away for that length of time now." Ashley assured him she didn't even think of him doing that. Jim said, "That's something to keep in mind though." Then Jim changed the subject by talking about his work there at K.U. in medical school and how interesting it was becoming. Then they each said to the other "I love you," and hung up.

The first thing Ashley did was call Janet and told her of her phone call. Janet was happy for her, not jealous, but wished she had something in her life besides her job. Janet said, "I wish I could meet your lovers." Ashley was astounded, she didn't think of it that way, but I guess that's the way it is. Ashley thought, *I really should share, but I don't know which one it would be, unless Chris, but how would they ever meet?* That was a good question, and she realized she didn't even want to share, and then her conscience really bothered her for being so selfish. Pastor Smucker wouldn't approve of that at all. She thought, *It's been so long. Jack probably has a lady friend and may even be serious with her, then that would narrow it down to two.* For an instant she wished that were true and thought the only way to find out is to call him.

Several weeks had gone by and Mary and Samantha were both home from college for their "spring break." They were in the midst of packing all their personal belongings as the house was sold. The farm and machinery all went for a good price that even astonished the Coopers. They were having a moving van to come in and pack all the furniture, dishes, and all their belongings. Mom and Dad Cooper found a large house in town to rent, as they were moving there to stay until their new house could be built. Janet and Ashley didn't know this yet. They'd no doubt want to come home to go through their personal belongings as well. Mom and Dad would call them both this evening to see if they can get off work for a week at least, as they both loved their jobs and would want to return afterwards.

They called Janet first and she was very surprised and excited. She told her folks just to take care of them for her if she couldn't get off work, which they promised they would do. Then they called Ashley and she nearly fainted at the news, to think the farm, house and all, were already sold, and they had a house in Abilene to move into already.

She said she hated to ask the Worths for time off already as she had been there only several months, but promised she would talk to them and let them know at once. Then, Ashley said, "I love you," and hung up.

Dinner was over, and things were in "tip top" shape, and she went downstairs and asked the Worths if they had time to talk. Of course, they said they did, and they hoped it wasn't anything about her job. Ashley said, "Yes and no." She told them everything and they said they went a long time without her, they could get along for as long as she had to be gone, but they sure wanted her to promise she would return. Ashley said she would be gone probably two weeks with the traveling and all. She said she would call Janet and see what the Sterlings said about her leaving. This she did. Janet told Ashley she was just ready to call her when the phone rang and that they had given her two weeks off but also they wanted her to promise she would be back. So both decided to go together, as soon as they could get a flight out. They would be leaving in two days on the United Airways, and fly during the day. Both the Worths and the Sterlings offered to take them to Los Angeles where they would leave from. So they decided they would take the Sterlings' Lincoln Continental and all would go. This thrilled the girls.

Both families said, "No more work here as you'll want to be packing and getting ready for the trip." The girls were both pleased and loved them even more. Ashley called her folks and told them what time they would arrive in Wichita as that was where they'd be. Mom and Dad were delighted and had the moving van come for their furniture and belongings in three weeks, so that would just work out fine. Mary and Samantha would have left by then, but promised to come home several days to see their sisters.

While Ashley was packing to leave, she wondered out

loud, "Will I be able to see Jim while I'm home? Oh, I just have to!"

The day was here for leaving. They all had to get up early to get to Los Angeles by seven o'clock. All were on time and picked up the Worths and Ashley, who were all ready to leave. Ashley and Janet both were excited, especially about leaving together. The plane was on time and both the Worths and Sterlings watched the plane take off and waited until it was out of sight; then they left for their homes. Ashley and Janet were so excited they talked until lunch was served by the stewardess. They had a nice meal and both were very hungry as they hadn't eaten much for two days. They were too excited to eat, and the Worths and Sterlings took both Ashley and Janet out to eat the last evening before they were to leave the next morning. Then they each ate very little because of excitement.

The stewardess announced they were about ready to land at Wichita airport. Ashley and Janet were toward the front, so they could get out easily. There they saw Mom and Dad Cooper waiting. They ran up and embraced each other, then they went to get their suitcases. They were eager to get home and talked all the way home about their jobs, and the people whom they worked for. Mom and Dad were happy that their daughters were so happy and they smiled at each other.

"Well, here we are," said Dad, but not for long, as they planned to move to the city in three weeks. When the girls walked into the house, they couldn't believe the clutter, boxes lying around with personal items in them, along with Mary and Samantha's personal things. Ashley asked about her car and if it was all right. Dad Cooper assured her it was just waiting for her to drive it. They sat around the table drinking cups of hot tea. They always like to do that.

Then Mom said, "Ashley, your ring is gone."

She said, "Yes, I told you about it." They remembered, and dropped the subject. Tea time was over, and they all went upstairs to their bedrooms.

Ashley and Janet talked a while and then Ashley said, "I really want to see Jim while I'm home." Janet was surprised and asked when she was going to call him and Ashley said, "Tomorrow." Then they got into their beds and drifted off to sleep. Morning came and the girls were up early, as they were used to doing that at their jobs in California. They dressed and went downstairs and Mom had breakfast on the table, as she heard they were up early.

After breakfast Ashley called Jim. He was in his room and answered the phone. Was he ever surprised and thrilled to know they were home for several weeks. Ashley told him all about their moving into Abilene and asked if she could see him some time soon. Jim said, "Yes, this evening." Ashley was excited and thrilled. She said that would be fine and asked him what time. He said, "the sooner, the better." So they decided on six o'clock. They said good-bye and hung up.

Janet was already going through her personal belongings, and then Ashley got started on hers too. Ashley announced to her folks that Jim was coming that evening at 6:00. They were surprised "so soon" after their arrival, but they said that was fine and asked if it was serious. She said it might be getting that way. They admonished her to be sure. This time, she knew what she was doing, and said, "You can be sure this time."

They were so busy that no one wanted to stop and eat lunch, but they did and were going out to eat this evening. Ashley said she would stay home to wait for Jim, which she did. Six o'clock was here and so was Jim, right on time. They kissed and hugged and said all the usual "love" things, and then Ashley told him they were going out to eat dinner, and it was on her. He said, "We'll see."

Amazingly, they walked in the restaurant where her folks and Janet were eating. It was a large table and they sat down with them. Ashley introduced Janet to Jim, as Mom and Dad already had met him. Janet went "Wow." They all laughed a little.

The waitress came over to their table and asked Jim and Ashley if they wanted menus. They said, "Yes, please." They were ready to leave, Mom, Dad, and Janet. Dad told the waitress to put theirs on the same bill. Jim thanked him. Now they were alone, and Ashley had a lot to tell Jim about her work and the people whom she worked for, and just went on and on.

Jim said, "Wait a minute, slow down." She said she was so excited and so glad to be home so she could see him. Jim said, "Ditto." Their meal was being served, so they thanked the waitress and began to eat. They ate hurriedly, and left. Jim put Ashley in the car on the driver's seat, then slid in beside her, as he was used to doing. Jim told Ashley when she called and said she was here, he knew he was going to ask her "for your hand in marriage."

She said, "Jim, I just ended one engagement and I'm not quite sure I want to be engaged again so soon."

Jim said, "Ashley, I don't want to let you go, ever!" She said she thought he was the one for her, as she loved him so much, and couldn't bear to be away from him when she was in California. But she felt she was doing the right thing now working as a maid, and she thoroughly enjoyed it. It was good training for when she did get married. Then the jeweler's shop was there at a stop sign, so he pulled in front of it and parked. Jim got out of the car, let Ashley out, and they went in. Jim told her he was going to buy her a locket to carry both their pictures in. Ashley was excited, and said, "Sure, I'd love to wear it." When they got in the car, he put the locket around her neck and decided when they would get pictures for it.

Jim said, "Ashley, this doesn't tie you down, just a reminder how much we love each other." She agreed. They were home now and Jim said he wouldn't go in because he'd better get back to K.U., so they gave each other a big squeeze and a passionate kiss, and he walked her to the door and left.

As she got into the house, Mom and Dad and Janet knew something had happened. Ashley informed them immediately, "No, we didn't get engaged, but look what I'm wearing, and we're getting our pictures taken before I leave for the West. It's a reminder of our love for each other." The family was happy for her.

When they said, "good night" and went upstairs to their rooms, Janet said, "Ashley, I like him a lot and I can't believe how handsome he is." She agreed.

The next morning came and around the breakfast table Ashley asked her folks and Janet, "What about Janet and I driving my car out West so I can have it there with me? I'm tired of depending on you, Janet, and I'm tired of taxi cabs." Mom and Dad looked at each other, then at Janet.

Janet said, "I'm game. That sounds like an excellent idea, but we'll have to leave earlier than we expected and we have round-trip tickets."

Dad said, "I'll buy them from you and maybe I can make a change on them and visit you out there after we're settled in our home in Abilene." Mom liked that idea very much. So it was settled to do just that. All four girls wanted to go into Abilene to see their home where they were going to rent until their new house was built. So Dad and Mom Cooper were taking them in tomorrow. They are also going to show them the site where their new house will be built.

This was exciting to them, they couldn't wait. Meantime, Jim and Ashley had an appointment to have their pictures to be taken for Ashley's locket. She was thrilled about that. They Each one of the girls had a pile of clothes of theirs, which they didn't want, after having gone through their belongings to be taken to "Goodwill." Mom Cooper was glad they were all there to do that, as she didn't want to be responsible for them. They were also relieved that the moving van was coming to pack all the dishes and other breakables with the furniture, so they pretty much had everything under control. It was good they had a place in town to move into because the people who bought the place wanted to move into it in three weeks, and they would be out in time.

Everything worked well for the Coopers. Ashley and Janet were really glad that they came back home for two weeks to be caught up on everything and could even drive Ashley's car back. Ashley pretty much knew Jim was the one whom she loved the most and the one who she later would marry. Maybe they'd discuss that when they went to have their pictures taken for the locket. She hoped Jim would bring it up.

A letter came in that mail for Ashley. It was from Jack Riley from Ohio. Ashley tore it open hurriedly and then went upstairs to read it. She wondered what he would be writing for. The letter began: "My dearest Ashley, I hope you'll forgive me for writing you after you told me you wanted to discontinue corresponding. I can't get you off of my mind: I'm so in love with you," and it went on about how she was doing and her "love life." Ashley couldn't believe what she was reading, but there it was in black and white. Then Jack ended his letter by saying, "If you'll just let me know how you're doing, I'll be grateful, Love, Jack."

In a way Ashley was outraged by him taking so much

for granted and in another sense, she was excited that he loved her so much. Then she thought, *Now what do I do. He'll expect an answer.* Maybe if she told him she'd found the one whom she was going to marry, maybe once and for all, he'd leave her alone. She really felt as if she was beginning to love only one out of the three and she was thankful for that. She felt love has, and is going from Chris, and she hasn't heard from him since the telephone call she made to him from California. She also figured she would wait to write to him until she gets back west. Then this was haunting her. She wondered how long it would be before she and Jim could get married. She hoped when she saw him to get pictures taken that Jim would bring up the subject. Oh, she hoped he would.

Just then Janet yelled upstairs, "Ashley, lunch is on the table." So she went down and hoped no one would suspect anything was wrong.

But no, she couldn't keep it hidden, and she blurted out, "I got a letter from Jack Riley from Ohio today," and she disclosed nearly everything that was in the letter. They were all aghast. She told them not to be too shocked because at one time she had loved all three men the same way, but really now she felt love was disappearing from Jack and also Chris.

They thanked her for telling them this, and Dad Cooper said, "Now I believe my little girl is growing up and getting wise." Ashley thanked him for that.

She told them this was the way she was thinking: "If Chris and Jack would marry I could live with that, but if Jim would marry, I wouldn't like that at all." She said that was the reason she felt like Jim was the one she honestly loved. She also said that this locket almost meant as much as an engagement ring would, and that she was never going to take it off. This thrilled her Mom and Dad. Also it made

Janet feel like she meant it from her heart, and she told Ashley so.

Several days had come and gone and this was the day Jim and Ashley were going to get pictures taken for Ashley's locket. She was excited and almost couldn't wait. But wait she did. Jim's car just drove up in the driveway. She grabbed her purse and ran out to his car.

Jim said, "Wait a minute, you are in a hurry, aren't you?" She gave a shy smile as if to say "Indeed, I am." She got in on her own on the driver's seat. Jim said, "Whoa, my girl is in a hurry to get these pictures taken." She announced she was.

The pictures turned out great. They were both delighted. Jim said, "I haven't gotten my kiss yet today."

Ashley said, "I've been waiting all afternoon." He pulled over to the side of the road and they kissed passionately.

Jim said, "It will be a while, but I'm ready to marry you now."

Ashley said, "What about my job in California?"

Jim said, "You could be my maid in our home."

Ashley was startled, then said, "Jim, will it be a long time before we can marry?"

Jim said, "I didn't tell you this for no reason at all, but I have wealthy parents, and they want to pay for my tuition. I wanted to do this on my own, but if we would get married, I'm sure they would help us out." Then he turned to Ashley and said, "Honey, will you be my bride and live with me forever?"

She said, "Jim I got a letter yesterday from Jack Riley and he said he loves me so much and I was shocked he would write after I broke off our correspondence. You know I broke my engagement to Chris, and I recently decided for sure if I would marry, it would be one hundred percent to you because I love you more than I do the other two who have been in my life, but they're not any more. I was going to write Jack when I get back to California and tell him it's over for him and me because I fell deeply in love with Jim Bennington, and I'm sure he's the one for me." Jim put his arms around her and squeezed her and kissed her again. Ashley said, "It sounds like I'm proposing, doesn't it?"

Then Jim said, "It saves me from having to do it. Ashley, I couldn't bear it if you married another man. I'd be crushed." Jim said, "Honey, whenever, it's forever."

Ashley threw her arms around his neck and said, "Oh, yes Jim, whenever, it's forever."

Then they both were so happy that they started for Ashley's home. Jim was driving with one hand, with his other one around Ashley. They both knew in their hearts it's forever, whenever! They were rather quiet the rest of the way home, but each could tell the other's happiness. They knew this was the last time they would see each other, as Ashley and Janet were leaving for California in several days. They were both hoping it wouldn't be too long, but Ashley knew in her heart it was at last settled and no other love, only Jim. She said to herself, *it was worth the trip home.*

When she got inside the house, her family was eating dinner. She sat down with them but was too happy and excited to eat. The one thing she was going to do was call Pastor Smucker and tell him the good news, but first she showed the locket to her Mom and Dad and Janet. They had never seen her happier than when she was now, so they knew in their minds it was settled. Pastor Smucker was so happy about Ashley's news. He never even had a doubt in his mind but that it was true and said, "Ashley, God bless you and Jim."

Mary and Samantha both finished college and had

careers of their own. Mom and Dad Cooper were living in their new house. Ashley and Janet drove back to California and worked for the Sterlings and the Worths. Ashley never heard what became of Chris and Jack, but she felt in her heart that they too, were doing all right and happy. Ashley quit working for the Worths as she and Jim were married after two years. Jim is an "intern" now and in several more years will be practicing medicine, while Ashley is a flight attendant for United Airways and both will continue to live happily ever after.